sink trap

Berkley Prime Crime titles by Christy Evans

SINK TRAP
LEAD-PIPE CINCH
DRIP DEAD

drip
dead

christy evans

BERKLEY PRIME CRIME, NEW YORK

THE BERKLEY PUBLISHING GROUP
Published by the Penguin Group
Penguin Group (USA) Inc.
375 Hudson Street, New York, New York 10014, USA
Penguin Group (Canada), 90 Eglinton Avenue East, Suite 700, Toronto, Ontario M4P 2Y3, Canada
(a division of Pearson Penguin Canada Inc.)
Penguin Books Ltd., 80 Strand, London WC2R 0RL, England
Penguin Group Ireland, 25 St. Stephen's Green, Dublin 2, Ireland (a division of Penguin Books Ltd.)
Penguin Group (Australia), 250 Camberwell Road, Camberwell, Victoria 3124, Australia
(a division of Pearson Australia Group Pty. Ltd.)
Penguin Books India Pvt. Ltd., 11 Community Centre, Panchsheel Park, New Delhi—110 017, India
Penguin Group (NZ), 67 Apollo Drive, Rosedale, North Shore 0632, New Zealand
(a division of Pearson New Zealand Ltd.)
Penguin Books (South Africa) (Pty.) Ltd., 24 Sturdee Avenue, Rosebank, Johannesburg 2196,
South Africa

Penguin Books Ltd., Registered Offices: 80 Strand, London WC2R 0RL, England

This is a work of fiction. Names, characters, places, and incidents either are the product of the author's imagination or are used fictitiously, and any resemblance to actual persons, living or dead, business establishments, events, or locales is entirely coincidental. The publisher does not have any control over and does not assume any responsibility for author or third-party websites or their content.

PUBLISHER'S NOTE: Neither the publisher nor the author is engaged in rendering professional advice or services to the individual reader. The ideas, projects, and suggestions contained in this book are not intended as a substitute for consulting with a professional. Neither the author nor the publisher shall be liable or responsible for any loss or damage allegedly arising from any information or suggestion in this book.

DRIP DEAD

A Berkley Prime Crime Book / published by arrangement with Tekno Books

PRINTING HISTORY
Berkley Prime Crime mass-market edition / February 2011

Copyright © 2011 by Penguin Group (USA) Inc.
Cover illustration by Brandon Dorman.
Cover design by Rita Frangie.
Interior text design by Laura K. Corless.

ISBN: 978-0-425-23989-6

BERKLEY® PRIME CRIME
Berkley Prime Crime Books are published by The Berkley Publishing Group,
a division of Penguin Group (USA) Inc.,
375 Hudson Street, New York, New York 10014.
BERKLEY® PRIME CRIME and the PRIME CRIME logo are trademarks of Penguin Group (USA) Inc.

PRINTED IN THE UNITED STATES OF AMERICA

10   9   8   7   6   5   4   3   2   1

To all the mothers and daughters in my life,
fighting and laughing and learning every day
what it means to be a family:
Jeanne, Jan, Jeri, Lynette, Petula, Zoe, and all the rest.
I love you.

acknowledgments

As always, thanks to my editors Michelle and Denise; my first reader and cheerleader, Colleen; husband and support system, Steve; and all my OWN buddies—especially Kris and Dean—for their friendship and moral support.

My gratitude also goes to Rita Frangie for her great covers, and an extra special shout-out to Brandon Dorman for his amazing artwork. I love those dogs!!

The aerator is the device on the tip of the faucet spout that mixes air and water. It can become clogged with dirt and minerals on the screen and disc and impede the movement of water in your faucet, so it needs to be cleaned regularly to maintain good water flow. Unscrew the aerator, using penetrating oil to loosen stubborn connections if needed. Disassemble the parts. If the screen or disc is damaged or clogged with mineral deposits, replace the parts—they're available cheaply at any home or hardware store. Otherwise, if they seem in good condition, clean the screen and disc with soapy water and a brush, and use a pin or toothpick to open clogged holes in the disc. Flush the parts with clean water and reassemble.

—A Plumber's Tip from Georgiana Neverall

chapter 1

I pointed the flashlight under my mother's house and looked around. A series of concrete footings stretched into the gloom outside the flashlight's beam, a heavy pier rising from each one to support the floor joists.

The high-powered beam cut through the darkness, throwing exaggerated shadows across the packed dirt beneath the house. It smelled damp, a mixture of dirt and heaven-knows-what-else that hadn't been disturbed in years.

And I was going to voluntarily crawl under there.

Of course I was. A plumber spends a lot of time under houses, and I was a plumber. Well, almost a plumber. Just as soon as I passed my licensing exam I would be the real deal.

So what was stopping me from crawling under Mom's house and checking out the foundation and the pipes?

The house was practically mine anyway. I'd agreed to buy it when Mom and Mr. Too-Smooth Gregory Whitlock got engaged and Mom had morphed into Pine Ridge, Oregon's, most demanding bride-to-be. I'd agreed to be her maid of honor ("You really should be a matron of honor at your age, Georgiana, but since you refuse to get married . . ."). Then she announced she was moving into Gregory's home, and offered to sell me her house, the house where I grew up.

Half of Mom's stuff had already gone to Gregory's. Even if I didn't want to think about it, I knew she was probably sleeping at his house most every night.

Eeew!

They're adults.

It's perfectly normal.

They're getting married.

All the arguments I'd given my sometimes boyfriend, Wade, when he talked about his mother dating again after her divorce rang in my head. But this was different. This was *my* mother. Completely different situation. Completely.

Was I having second thoughts about buying the house? Was that why I was stalling? Barry Hickey of Hickey & Hickey Plumbing—aka my boss—said it was a good deal, but could he be sure? How much did he really know about the condition of the house?

There was only one way to find out.

I pulled a mask over my nose and mouth, blocking out the musty smell that seeped from the crawl space, and wiggled through the opening. I wanted to get this over with before Sandra Neverall—mother, bridezilla extraordinaire, and doyenne of Whitlock Estates Realty—came home and decided to supervise.

I tried to get my bearings, mentally picturing the floor plan above my head. To the far right was a wall that divided the house from the garage. On this side of that wall was the kitchen.

I could start there.

I crawled between the footings, my flashlight casting a narrow line of bright light in the darkness. Cold seeped up from beneath me, penetrating the heavy denim of my coveralls. The calendar might say it was summer, but the dirt under the house hadn't got that memo.

The pipes under the kitchen were galvanized steel, no surprise given the age of the house. There was no way to know what shape they were in, since they corroded from the inside out, but the life expectancy of galvanized was only about thirty years.

I would likely be replacing pipes in the near future.

I scribbled a few notes in a small notebook and stuffed it back in the breast pocket of my coveralls. This was one place I agreed with Barry. A pencil and paper were the best tools for the job—I wouldn't want to drag electronic gizmos under a house with me.

I turned left, moving slowly between the footings, imagining the rooms above my head. I moved under the dining room, toward the living room, bedrooms, and bathroom beyond.

Up ahead, about where I thought the hallway should be, a sliver of light caught my eye. I doused the flashlight for a minute, letting my eyes adjust to the low light. Sure enough, there was a narrow band of light in the floor above, outlining a square about three feet on a side.

On the dirt below the strip of light there was a deeper shadow. A large box, maybe. Had mom stored something under the house? As far as I knew, everything was stacked neatly in labeled boxes in the attic.

What was down here in the cold and damp?

I turned the flashlight back on and worked my way toward the object. In the beam of the flashlight I could see that it was several smallish boxes stacked on top of one another.

Something stuck out from one end of the pile of boxes. It wasn't another box; the shape was irregular, though most of it was hidden from sight behind the stacked boxes.

The crawl space was more than musty, and I was grateful for the small protection of the face mask. I had the sinking feeling I was going to find a small deceased animal somewhere in my travels, judging by the odor that seeped under the mask.

I was close enough now to see that the boxes were wooden shipping crates. Only a couple feet on each side, they could easily have been lowered through the opening faintly outlined above.

My curiosity was piqued. I wanted to know what was in those crates, and why they were hidden under the house

I was buying—my mom's house and my old family home.

It was like a buried treasure.

I suppose I could have crawled back out and called Mom to ask her what this was all about, but I didn't want to wait for an answer, or give her another chance to discuss every minute detail of the wedding. Why couldn't she just elope to Reno or Las Vegas?

I got close enough to make out a shipping label on one box. It was addressed to Gregory, my soon-to-be stepfather, with a return address in Paris—France, not Texas.

A shiver ran through me. I couldn't think of a single good reason for Gregory to get a shipment from outside the country and hide it under my mother's house.

I could think of several bad reasons.

I wondered if my mother might have a big problem.

Then I realized I was kidding myself. Just because Gregory wasn't the man I'd choose for Mom to marry, it didn't mean he was running guns or hiding nukes.

I moved to one side, trying to guess how many boxes were stacked under the house.

I shined my flashlight over the scene in front of me, trying to make sense of what I saw. Something didn't look right, no matter how I moved the light or turned my head.

I heard a scream. It took a few seconds to realize it came from me.

Mom's problem just got a lot bigger.

The lumpy shape behind the boxes was Gregory Whitlock.

And I was pretty sure he was dead.

chapter 2

I clamped my mouth shut, cutting off the scream. Instead I started to whimper. That didn't help, either.

I should check for a pulse. Maybe Gregory just fell and he was hurt. Or stuck. He didn't have to be dead.

I crawled a little closer. My heart pounded so hard I was sure it would burst right out of my chest, and I couldn't seem to hold the flashlight steady. The beam flickered crazily over the scene in front of me.

Gregory wore a pair of neatly pressed khakis, a crisp oxford cloth shirt in pale blue, and expensive penny loafers. Casual but not sloppy. The shoes were nearly new, the soles facing me were still unmarked by wear.

I didn't want to touch him.

I stretched my arm, holding the flashlight out in front of me, and tapped it against his left foot.

No response.

He hadn't reacted to my screaming, either.

I backed away from Gregory and the boxes. Within a few feet I ran into one of the concrete footings. I had to turn around to watch where I was going as I made my way toward the access hole.

My stomach clenched and my breath came in gasps. I felt as if there was something lurking in the dark corners. Something big and bad. Something I had to get away from.

Panic pushed me forward.

I reached the opening to the outside world and clambered through it. The tool loop at my right hip caught on a corner. I tugged to free myself and escape from the crawl space.

From whatever was hiding down there.

Logically I knew there was nothing under the house. But logic and fear don't mix, and right then fear was definitely in charge.

I ran in the back door and grabbed my cell phone from the kitchen table.

I punched 9-1-1 into the cell and tried to calm my breathing as I waited for the emergency operator to answer.

I somehow managed to explain my situation to the man who answered. I probably wasn't very coherent, but I don't really remember much of the conversation. He kept me on the phone while he talked to the fire department and local sheriff's office, assured me someone would be there within a few minutes, and kept talking calmly to me while we waited.

I wondered if the dispatcher was anyone I knew. I'd met a lot of the local deputies over the last several months. Maybe it was one of them. I tried to remember their names.

Anything to avoid thinking about what was under the house.

In the distance I heard sirens.

"Are there trucks coming?" I asked the operator. "I can hear sirens."

"That should be them," he answered. "There aren't any other calls in the area. Are you okay to wait for them now?"

I swallowed hard. "I, uh, I think so," I managed to lie.

"They're just a couple streets away. If you go outside, you should be able to see them coming."

I walked to the front door, bumping into furniture as if I had never been in the house before. When I stepped outside, the sirens sounded very close. And very loud.

The operator spoke, but it was impossible to understand him over the wails of the sirens.

"They're here," I said, seeing a rescue unit come around a corner a couple blocks away. "I have to go."

There was a noise from the other end of the phone that I assumed was the operator signing off. I hung up and slipped the phone in my pocket.

The square box on wheels with "Pine Ridge Medic Unit" on the front was one of the most beautiful things I had ever seen.

The rescue unit pulled to the curb in front of the house and two men in navy blue uniforms jumped out.

One of the men started taking boxes and supplies from the back of the truck while the other one ran toward me.

"This way," I said, leading him along the side of the garage. There was a gate at the back. I figured it would be easier to get their equipment through there instead of having to drag it through the house.

"You said there was someone under the house?"

"It's Gregory. Gregory Whitlock. He's my mother's fiancé. This is her house. Well, I mean, it's my house, almost. I'm buying it from her but she still lives here until the wedding—"

I stopped in the middle of the yard.

Wedding!

The groom-to-be was under the house. Dead.

There wasn't going to be any wedding.

Someone had to tell my mother.

Whoa.

That someone was probably going to be me.

"Miss?" The paramedic was looking at me and it was clear he had spoken before. I had been lost in my own little nightmare. And it was only beginning.

I showed him where the access hole was. He played his high-powered flashlight under the house, lighting the space up a lot more than mine had.

"That direction," I said, pointing toward where the boxes had been. "Toward the front."

He nodded. By now his partner had joined him and they quickly donned protective jumpsuits and breathing gear. "Does this house have gas heat?"

I shook my head. "All electric. Why?"

I remembered my mother grumbling about electric rates and how she could barely afford to heat the place.

"Want to be sure the problem isn't a gas leak. Dispatch said there wasn't gas to the house, but I like to be sure."

He lowered his face mask and followed his partner under the house.

I could hear them scuffing along in the narrow crawl space. I could follow their progress by the movement of the flashlight beam. They were getting close.

"Miss Neverall."

It wasn't a question, it was a statement.

I stood up quickly from where I was crouched, watching the progress of the paramedics, and found myself looking up into the face of Fred Mitchell, the sheriff of Pine Ridge.

I knew he'd told me to call him Fred, since he was dating my best friend, but I was certain this wasn't a good time for that. "Hello, Sheriff."

The sheriff glanced around as though he expected to see someone else appear. When no one did, he turned his attention back to me. "Care to tell me what happened here?"

I explained that I was buying the house from my mother, and I wanted to make an assessment of the structure. I was just getting to the part about checking the plumbing when he interrupted me.

"That's all very interesting," he said in a tone that implied it quite clearly was not, "but what happened?"

He pulled a small notebook from his pocket and started writing. "You were the one who called 9-1-1, correct?"

"Yes."

"And you said there was someone under the house and you thought he might be dead."

I nodded, suddenly unable to actually speak. I did think Gregory was dead, but it was the first time anyone had actually said the word.

"Did you recognize the man? You told the dispatcher you knew him."

"It was Gregory. Gregory Whitlock. My mother's fiancé, and I don't know what he was doing down there—besides maybe being dead, I mean—and I don't know how he got there, or anything, and there isn't anything I can tell you."

My voice was rising in pitch, the words tumbling out faster and faster. I could feel panic taking control. My hands shook, and my legs refused to hold me up for a second longer.

I sat down on the wet grass, adding grass stains to the dirt and damp from the crawl space. It didn't matter. I was going to burn these coveralls just as soon as I could take them off.

"Georgie?" Sheriff Mitchell crouched next to me, and put a hand on my arm. "Are you okay?"

Why did people even ask that question when it was abundantly clear someone was not okay and would not be okay for a long time?

"No," I said softly. "I'm not. I just found a man under the house I am buying, the house where my mother lives. I think he's"—I swallowed hard and forced the word out of my mouth—"dead. I know who he is, and he's supposed to marry my mother in a few weeks. I am definitely not okay."

chapter 3

Sheriff Mitchell suggested we sit in his car to talk. He offered me his hand and helped me to my feet. The paramedics were under the house and an additional crew arrived as the sheriff was opening the car for me.

I slid into the front seat.

My coveralls were filthy, and I started to apologize.

Sherriff Mitchell shook his head. "Not a problem, Georgie. If you just wait here a minute, I need to talk to the paramedics."

He hurried away without waiting for my answer.

Next door, Mrs. Sweeney peeked out her kitchen window that overlooked Mom's driveway. All she could see from there were the three emergency vehicles now clustered in front of the house, and the sheriff talking with the newly arrived paramedics.

I turned in the seat to look in the other direction.

Sure enough, I saw a curtain hastily dropped back in place at the Gordens' house across the street, and a few doors down Harry Hamilton stood on his porch with a coffee mug in his hand, openly staring at the accumulation of vehicles and emergency workers in front of Mom's house.

Sheriff Mitchell returned in a couple minutes and slid

behind the wheel. His expression was grim, confirming what I had known from the instant I had seen Gregory under the house.

He looked at me and shook his head. "We'll need to talk to your mother. Do you know where we can reach her?"

Someone was going to have to tell my mother. It was going to be bad. She'd already been a widow once and now it was happening again. Only this time it was before the wedding.

The coffee and granola bar I'd eaten for breakfast chose that moment to revolt.

I yanked the car door open, grateful to be in the front seat where there were door handles. I didn't make it completely out of the car, but I leaned away from the door as I emptied the contents of my stomach onto the shoulder.

I swiped my sleeve across my mouth and struggled for control. There was nothing left inside me, but that didn't stop my stomach from trying to turn itself inside out.

The sheriff waited patiently for me to sit back up. When I did he handed me a tissue from a box under the dash, and a small bottle of water. "I can't let you go in the house to get a drink right now," he explained apologetically. "Not until we know what happened."

I nodded my understanding and accepted the tissue and the water. I rinsed my mouth and spit, then took a tiny sip.

The water wasn't chilled, but it felt cool as it slid down my throat and coated my burning stomach. I wiped my mouth and turned back to face the sheriff.

"Sorry," I muttered, embarrassed by the rebellion of my stomach.

"It happens." The sheriff's voice was calm, with a note of professional concern. "Feel better?"

I nodded without speaking. The spasms had subsided, though I was still shaky. And there was still the problem of telling my mother.

"Do you know where your mother is?" The sheriff didn't sound pleased with the prospect of talking to Sandra

Neverall, and I didn't blame him. They had crossed paths several months earlier, when he had questioned me about the death of Blake Weston.

Neither one of them had enjoyed the encounter.

I tried to access the information that was jumbled in my brain. I was doing my checking while Mom was gone. I knew she was gone. She told me where—if I could just remember . . .

"Gregory's," I groaned. "She was taking things to Gregory's house."

He started the engine. "Do you think she'll still be there? How long ago did she leave?"

I shook my head as I fastened my seat belt. "I don't know. I talked to her a couple hours ago, I guess. She was going to Gregory's to take some of her things over. She didn't say exactly what, and I didn't ask.

"She might still be there or she might be at the office. Or somewhere else entirely."

"Can you call her?" he asked. "Don't do it if you can't handle it," he added hastily. "It's bad enough we have to give her the news. I would much rather we do it in person."

"I can try," I said doubtfully. I pulled my phone out of my pocket and began searching through the directory for Mom's cell phone number. I usually knew it better than I knew my own. But not right now.

The sheriff picked up the radio and talked softly to dispatch, asking for the address of Gregory Whitlock's residence.

But before he could get a reply, the question became moot.

Two blocks away a Cadillac Escalade rounded the corner. Then it shot toward us at high speed. At the last second, the driver braked hard and screeched to a stop only inches from the front of the sheriff's car.

Mom jumped from the front seat, and stormed over to the sheriff's door.

"What is the meaning of this?" she demanded. "Why do you have my daughter in your police car? Again?"

"Mrs. Neverall, please—" the sheriff began in a conciliatory tone.

"Don't try to soft soap me!" she snapped. "Harry Hamilton called me the minute you forced Georgiana into your car! You let her out this instant."

She looked around, taking in the collection of emergency vehicles, and the rescue and fire personnel coming and going through the open gate to her backyard.

"And you had better have a damned good explanation for this violation of my daughter's rights and my property!"

Who was this woman? My mother never screamed at people, she never swore, and she had taught me that a lady never made a scene in public.

Of course, she had never had a neighbor call and describe her daughter being shoved into a police car, either. And if I knew Harry Hamilton, the whole story had been expanded and embellished beyond recognition.

"Mother." I opened the door and stood up. My legs threatened to give way, and I leaned heavily against the car. "Mother, please. The sheriff and I were simply talking. He *helped* me into the car like a proper gentleman. Nobody forced me."

As I spoke, the sheriff opened his door and climbed out. He took my mother by the arm and guided her toward the front of the house.

"Why don't we all go somewhere private?" he asked. He shot me a look of gratitude, as though thanking me for intervening, before he turned his attention back to my mother. "We need to talk, Mrs. Neverall."

I could see my mother wavering. She didn't want to let the sheriff tell her what to do, but she clearly was curious about what was going on. I wished we didn't have to satisfy that curiosity.

"Come on, Mom," I said quietly. I reached for her keys and looked questioningly at the sheriff.

He nodded to the garage, and I pushed the button to open the door. At least we could get out of the line of sight of the neighbors before this conversation went any further.

I led the way into the garage, where Gregory's latest car sat—a big, flashy Mercedes sedan that still carried the paper dealer registration stuck to the window. I flinched at the sight of the car, but my mother didn't notice. Her attention was focused on the sheriff, and you could almost see the steam rising off her.

Mom's stiletto heels tapped angrily across the carefully swept concrete. "I'm waiting for an explanation, Mitchell," she said, deliberately using his last name without the title of sheriff. She crossed her arms over her chest and stared at him.

If she intended to intimidate him it didn't work.

I glanced around and spotted some folding lawn chairs in the corner of the garage. The webbing had faded to a uniform gray, and the aluminum frames were pitted with dark spots of corrosion.

Mom would certainly refuse to voluntarily put the seat of her pale yellow linen pantsuit anywhere near the dirty-looking webbing, but her reactions might well be anything but voluntary.

I dragged a couple of the chairs out into the empty space where Mom usually parked her car and offered one to her and one to the sheriff.

She just glared at the decrepit-looking furniture and continued standing in the middle of the garage.

The sheriff shook his head slightly. He shifted nervously from one foot to the other as I positioned myself next to my mother. I kept one hand on the lawn chair in case my mother needed it.

"Mrs. Neverall," the sheriff said in a low voice, "this is about Gregory Whitlock. Your daughter found him in the crawl space under your house here.

"I'm very sorry, Mrs. Neverall, but Mr. Whitlock is dead."

Mom sat down in the ratty chair.

She didn't speak. She didn't cry, or scream, or argue with the sheriff that he much be mistaken. She simply collapsed into the chair I held ready, like a marionette with all her strings cut.

Over the years, I had dealt with Mom in many different moods. She was by turns bossy, condescending, judgmental, and angry. She could also be charming, witty, and persuasive. She was never at a loss for words.

Until now.

When Dad died, she had grieved openly and buried the bitterness and anger that came with the discovery of the debts he'd left behind.

It wasn't until his sudden heart attack that she had learned why the beloved Dr. Neverall was so beloved: if a patient was having a tough time, he simply didn't bill them. IIis death left her with a mountain of debt and a load of resentment. She had maintained the perfect public image of the heartbroken widow and in some ways she really was.

But now, sitting limply in the battered garden chair, she was a complete stranger. A woman I didn't know.

The silence stretched eerily for a couple minutes. The sheriff waited patiently for Mom to respond, as though he had all the time in the world.

Outside, the voices of the emergency crew rose and fell as they went past the garage on their way in and out of the backyard. Somewhere a block or two away someone was cutting grass, and the sound of the mower echoed in the silent garage.

I crouched down next to my mother and looked up into her face. Her eyes were dry, and she stared at the floor without blinking.

Was she in shock? I didn't know the symptoms well enough to be sure.

I looked up at the sheriff. "Do you think we ought to have one of the paramedics come take a look at her?"

He nodded and went out. The paramedics weren't in a hurry dealing with Gregory after all. They would have plenty of time to look at Mom and try to help her.

Gregory needed a coroner, not medical attention.

chapter 4

A dark-eyed paramedic with a military-style buzz cut followed the sheriff back into the garage. He crouched next to me and pulled a blood-pressure cuff and stethoscope from his kit.

Talking gently to Mom, as though she were a small child, the paramedic checked her over. He wrapped the cuff around her arm, all the while keeping up a steady stream of verbal reassurances.

When we finished, he stood up and nodded to me to follow.

We moved nearer to the sheriff, and the paramedic reported. "Medically she's fine. No indication of physical distress or trauma." He turned to me. "You're the daughter?"

I nodded.

"Did she know the deceased well?"

It took me a minute to process his question. It was the first time I had heard anyone refer to Gregory as "the deceased."

"They were engaged," I answered after a pause.

"That would do it." He glanced at Mom, who hadn't moved. She hadn't even looked up to see where we were. "The psychological shock was too great, and she's shut down. It may last a few minutes, or hours. Or it could go on for several days. There is no immediate medical reason to transport her to the hospital, but you might want to have her own doctor look at her later. She shouldn't be alone."

I nodded.

The sheriff hesitated. "How long before they can get Whitlock out of there?" he asked.

The paramedic shrugged. "Not long. But there's a pile of boxes under there, and the space is tight. Might be another thirty or forty minutes."

Sheriff Mitchell furrowed his brow. "Tell you what, Georgie. Take your mom over to see Doc Cox right now. He is her doctor, right?"

I nodded. It seemed to be all I was capable of at the moment.

"I'll call and let him know you're on the way. He should still be at Immediate Care," he said, checking his watch. "When you're done, I'll still need a formal statement from you." An ironic tone crept into his voice. "You should know that drill by now."

I couldn't argue with him. I'd already been dragged into the investigation of two murders in Pine Ridge, and my visits to the sheriff's office had become all too familiar.

Neither the sheriff nor I was happy about it.

"I'll call you as soon as we're through at the doctor's," I said before he could continue. "I don't know if I'll be able to leave her for a while, but I'm sure we can make some arrangement for you to take my statement. I can call a friend in to sit with her. But there isn't really much to tell, Sheriff. I came over to inspect the pipes, crawled under the house, and there he was."

I anticipated his next question and answered without being asked. "I didn't touch anything except his shoe. I kind of poked him to see if he would respond. When he didn't, I got out of there as fast as I could and called you."

Mitchell shook his head. "Still going to need a formal statement."

"I know." I sighed. "Just let me take care of my mom, okay?"

"Go on," he said. He reached for his radio and talked to the dispatcher, asking her to put him through to Dr. Cox.

I took Mom by the arm and led her out of the garage to her car. I opened the passenger door of her Escalade, and she climbed in. Harry Hamilton was still out on his porch, and I resisted the impulse to give him a one-fingered salute.

The Escalade roared to life, and I pulled away from the curb. I was used to driving my thirty-year-old Beetle and, sitting up high in the Escalade, I felt as though I were piloting a small continent. I had to admit it was a lot cushier than my Beetle. I bet the heater even worked.

I managed to navigate the huge vehicle to the Immediate Care Clinic without forcing anyone off the road. I even got it into a parking space. But getting the doors open wide enough to get out without denting the neighboring cars was a struggle.

Dr. Cox was expecting us, and the receptionist immediately showed us into an exam room.

I wondered if Mom was ever going to say anything. She hadn't spoken since Sheriff Mitchell had given her the news about Gregory. Mom never had trouble expressing her thoughts. Never. It was starting to creep me out.

"Mom? I'm really sorry, Mom."

"You never liked him." Her voice croaked when she spoke as though she had forgotten how to use it.

"Not much," I admitted. There was no reason to argue with her. She was right. "Still, he was important to you—"

I stopped as Dr. Cox came into the room.

"Hello," he said. He glanced my way before focusing on my mom. "How are you doing, Mrs. Neverall?" He walked over and took her hand, gently turning it over and pressing his fingertips against her wrist.

"I, well, I don't know," she admitted slowly.

"Sheriff Mitchell told me what happened," he reassured

her. "I'm very sorry." He held a stethoscope to her chest. "Deep breath."

She sucked in air, her breath catching in a sudden hiccup that seemed to break something loose in her chest. She held the breath for a moment as Dr. Cox moved the stethoscope, but when he said, "Breathe out," what escaped was a ragged sob.

The doctor caught her as she crumpled forward, tears running down her face. He looked at me over her head. I moved closer and Dr. Cox transferred Mom into my arms. I patted her back, not knowing what else to do.

We stayed that way for a couple minutes, until Mom drew a deep breath and shook herself free of my embrace.

"My apologies, Doctor," she said stiffly. She took the tissue the doctor offered and wiped delicately at her eyes. "Please forgive my outburst."

"Certainly, Sandra. It's a perfectly normal reaction." He placed the stethoscope back against her chest. "Okay. Breathe in."

Dr. Cox spent several minutes with Mom, examining her and talking to her. By the time he was through, my mother was once again her usual controlled—and controlling—self.

"May I have my keys, please?" she asked as we left the Immediate Care Clinic. She held out her freshly manicured hand. Plum Crazy. It was a perfect color for my mother—it described exactly how she made me feel.

I turned over the keys and climbed into the passenger's seat of the Escalade. I wasn't sure she should be driving, but I wasn't anxious to get behind the wheel of that beast again. And my car was at her house.

When we pulled up in front of her house, the ambulance was gone but the sheriff was still there. At least it would save me a phone call. His car was parked where Mom had found us, and several other cars were parked nearby. Yellow crime-scene tape was stretched across the gate, where a deputy stood guard with a clipboard.

As we climbed from the car, I saw the deputy writing notes. Another deputy came out of the backyard and stopped to sign the clipboard.

Before we could reach the door to the house, Sheriff Mitchell appeared from the backyard and intercepted us on the front lawn.

"You can't go in there, ladies."

"I most certainly can, Sheriff. This is my house." Yep, Mom was definitely back to her usual self.

"This is a crime scene, Mrs. Neverall. No one is allowed in until we have finished our investigation."

Color drained from Mom's face, and for an instant I was afraid she was going to shut down again. But she recovered quickly, drawing herself up straight. "Crime scene? My house? I find that hard to believe."

The sheriff shrugged off her objection. "Until we know how Mr. Whitlock died and what he was doing under your house, it's a crime scene and no one is allowed in."

He gave me a quick glance and I thought there was a hint of amusement in his eyes. He'd dealt with my mother before and he knew it wasn't often anyone got the upper hand with her. The gleam of humor disappeared so fast I couldn't be sure I'd really seen it, and he resumed speaking.

"Mrs. Neverall, do you have someplace else to stay? I really can't let you in the house."

Mom shook her head in disgust. "I've already started moving, so I guess I can just stay at Gregory's . . ." Her voice trailed off as she realized what she had said, and she studied the sheriff's face. "No, I suppose that's out, too, isn't it?"

The sheriff nodded. "Someplace else, maybe?"

I'd been backed into a trap, and we all knew it. With as much grace as I could muster, I said, "She can stay with me."

Mom looked horrified at the prospect, but there wasn't much she could say. It was that or stay somewhere out of town. There wasn't a real hotel in Pine Ridge, and the local bed and breakfast certainly wasn't up to her standards. Besides, she wasn't about to admit to anyone in town that she didn't have a place to stay.

The negotiations for Mom's move continued for several minutes. She demanded to pack her clothes, the sheriff refused. Eventually they settled on giving her ten minutes' access to her dresser and closet, under the supervision of one of Mitchell's deputies.

Mom wasn't happy with the arrangement, especially since there were no female deputies to oversee her packing, but eventually the sheriff gave her a take-it-or-leave-it choice and she capitulated.

I didn't wait for her to pack and follow me back to my house. Instead I climbed into the driver's seat of the Beetle and drove as fast as I dared to my rental house.

I only had a few minutes to prepare for Mom's visit.

I had to work fast.

I had a mess of my own to tackle before Mom walked through my door.

Water damage is one of the most expensive problems that can crop up in your home. One way to keep from being taken by surprise is to buy several small, battery-operated moisture alarms and put them in places that are likely to have small leaks that aren't easy to see— by the water heater, behind the toilets, under the sinks, and so on. Pick them up when you clean, and replace them when the floor is dry and they'll last for years. You'll hear an ear-splitting alarm at the first sign of trouble and can get a plumber in before thousands of dollars' worth of water damage has occurred.

—A Plumber's Tip from Georgiana Neverall

chapter 5

Daisy and Buddha greeted me at the door, anxious for a treat and a walk. I told them that even Airedales took second place to Mom right now and shooed them out into the backyard.

I threw myself into a cleaning frenzy. The house would never meet Sandra Neverall's exacting standards of domestic achievement, but I could at least scrape off a couple layers of chaos before she arrived.

I stripped the bed and set out clean sheets. The bathroom was, thankfully, mostly clean. I ran a sponge over the sink and counter, and yanked the used towels off the towel bar.

By the time Mom's Escalade pulled into the driveway, I had managed to get the bathroom fully clean, the bed remade, and the dirty dishes stowed in the dishwasher. I glanced at my watch and grinned. She had stretched her ten minutes into half an hour. The deputy charged with watching her was probably nursing a monster headache. I bet she'd packed half her wardrobe.

As if to confirm my conclusion, Mom came up the walk pulling two roll-along suitcases, with a computer case hanging from one shoulder. No way she managed to pack all that in ten minutes.

I met her at the door and took one of the suitcases. I

rolled it back to the bedroom and left it at the foot of the freshly made bed.

"You don't have to give up your bedroom, Georgiana," she said crisply. "I can take the guest room." She glanced down the hall toward the closed door. "Is that it?"

I shook my head. "That's not a bedroom, Mom. It's where I work out. You go ahead." I waved toward the bed with a gesture that took in the whole room. "I can sleep on the couch for a few days."

I was already regretting my decision to offer her a place to stay. She had only been in the house three minutes and already I could feel my shoulders knotting.

Silently I said a little prayer that it would only be a few days. Any longer than that and I knew we would be at each other's throats.

Mom's eyebrow shot up. "You have a workout room? I am impressed. What kind of equipment do you have?"

Before I could stop her she swung the door wide. She stopped in the doorway, her mouth drawing into a thin line. She turned to stare at me, arching one eyebrow in a way she knew annoyed me.

"*This* is what you call a workout room?" She waved one hand dramatically. "It looks more like a *padded* room." She let the phrase hang in the air, the tight lift of her lips suggesting I might really need a padded room.

"You know my workouts are based in martial arts, Mom. We've talked about this before." I clamped my mouth shut. No sense starting an argument within her first quarter hour in my house. Not when I would have plenty of time to argue with her in the days—or, heaven forbid, weeks—to come.

I picked up the laundry basket I'd brought from the bedroom and began stacking the sort-of-folded shirts and underwear on the empty shelf in the closet.

I made a mental note to get a new pair of pajamas. I couldn't actually sleep on the couch in the buff—my usual practice—and Mom would never approve of my alternative of a worn-out T-shirt.

There was a more pressing matter however. My refrigerator was in its usual state: mostly empty. In spite of repeated vows to shop and eat healthier, I always fell back into the bad habits that came from my years of hundred-hour workweeks in the high-tech industry.

Without looking I could inventory the contents: a few bottles of microbrew, leftover pizza, and a plastic container full of condiment packets from various fast-food joints.

The cupboards weren't much better. I needed to do some grocery shopping if I didn't want Mom to take control of that, too.

"Why don't I give you a little time to get settled, Mom?" I led her back to the bedroom. "You can unpack—I emptied the dresser for you—while I go pick up some groceries."

Mom opened her mouth but I continued before she could get a word out. "I won't be long. Just go ahead and make yourself at home."

"We'll see."

I bit back the impulse to laugh manically. Mom was a control freak. She would not only make herself at home, she'd take over completely. The only question was how long it would take.

I grabbed my wallet and keys and whistled for the dogs. If I took them with me there would be one less thing for Mom to complain about when I returned.

As soon as I parked the Beetle I pulled out my cell phone and called my best friend, Sue Gibbons, at Doggy Day Spa. I needed help if I was going to survive Mom's invasion.

"You're coming to dinner tonight," I told her when she answered the phone. "No argument, okay?"

"Why would I argue?" Sue laughed. "I love Garibaldi's."

"No pizza. Sorry. I'm going to cook."

"Whoa. What's the occasion? And what should I bring?"

"No occasion," I lied. "And you don't have to bring anything. I'm thinking spaghetti and garlic bread. I can handle it."

"Six?" Sue asked.

"Works for me," I replied.

"Uh, Georgie? You don't just randomly decide to cook because it's Thursday. Is Wade coming? Should I call Fred?"

"No!" I shouted into the phone, then realized how strongly I'd reacted. "No, don't call Fred. I can't explain right now, but Wade won't be there. Just us girls. Okay?" I tried not to wince at the word *girl* and carefully avoided mentioning that there would be another "girl" at dinner.

I hesitated. I hadn't really expected to get away without telling her, and it really wasn't fair not to give her some advance warning that she was having dinner with Mom. And why.

"Okay," I said. "This is an emergency. And it's compli- cated. Listen, I'm at the grocery store. I really can't ex- plain this on the phone. I'll come by the spa on my way home. But I can't stay long if I'm going to cook."

I hung up before she could ask me anything else.

Twenty minutes later I pulled up in front of Doggie Day Spa, having set a personal power-shopping record for the grocery store. The front-end cargo space of the Beetle was packed with enough groceries to last me several weeks, or Mom and me a few days. Fast-food dining made groceries last a long time, but I knew that wasn't going to be possible with Mom in the house.

I let the dogs out of the car, clipping on their leashes. Sue met us at the door of her pet grooming shop with treats for the dogs and a question for me.

"What's going on, Georgie? When I tried to call Fred he wasn't available, and the deputy who took my message was acting awfully strange. That couldn't have anything to do with why you didn't want me to invite him to din- ner, could it?"

Her tone was curious, but there was an edge. She'd been dating the sheriff for a few months, and we occasionally double-dated: her and Fred, and me and Wade Montgom- ery, a Pine Ridge City Councilman and my sort-of boyfriend. But since I'd been involved in the investigation of a couple murders in Pine Ridge, Fred and I were sometimes at odds.

I motioned to a stool behind the counter, and Sue took the hint.

I still didn't know where to start, but there wasn't time to tiptoe around the truth. "Gregory Whitlock's dead."

Sue's mouth dropped open but no sound came out.

"I found him," I continued, "this morning." Had it only been a few hours ago? It felt like an eternity since those few horrible minutes under the house.

"You found him? Where was he?" Sue's voice strained with shock.

"He was under Mom's house." Even though it was the truth, I realized how absurd it sounded when I said it that way.

"What?"

I tried to explain. "I went to check the plumbing and stuff in the crawl space under the house. He was down there." I shrugged. "I don't know how he got there or what he was doing. In fact, I don't know much of anything about this. I just know he was dead."

"But, how . . .?"

I shrugged again. "Ask Fred. He isn't telling me—or Mom—anything. All I know is that he won't let my mother back in her house, and she can't stay at Gregory's, either."

Sue eyed me suspiciously. "And just where is she staying?"

"With me," I admitted miserably. "Which is why you have to come to dinner tonight. I left her unpacking, but I'm stuck with her until your boyfriend lets her back in her house, or lets her stay at Gregory's. I mean, she'd practically moved in there already, so she ought to be able to stay there, shouldn't she?"

I tried not to think about how long it might be before I could get Mom back into her own house. I already knew it wouldn't be soon enough.

"So you have to come to dinner," I pleaded. "Just for a

little while, to give me a break. Maybe, with you there, we can get through this evening with a little dignity intact."

Speaking of dignity, another thought occurred to me. "And do you have a pair of pajamas I can borrow? Just until I can get into town to buy some new ones." Pine Ridge wasn't known for its shopping opportunities.

Sue's brow furrowed. Usually she was the one on a conversational roller coaster. It took a second for the question to register, then she nodded. "Sandra won't approve of the ratty T-shirt, will she? I have a brand-new pair at home. I'll bring them with me."

She glanced over at the dogs, settled contentedly in their favorite nap spots, and shook her head. "The pups could use a brushing. Why don't you leave them here and go deal with Sandra? I owe you for the last round of computer work and I can bring them with me at six."

She looked around the empty shop. "Pretty quiet here this afternoon, anyway."

I couldn't hide the relief I felt. I wished, for Sue's sake, the shop was busier, but I was grateful for her willingness to take Daisy and Buddha off my hands for the afternoon.

She did owe me for some computer maintenance I'd done for her. Not many people in Pine Ridge knew I'd owned a computer security firm in San Francisco, but the ones who did—like Sue and my boss, Barry Hickey—were happy to take advantage of my expertise.

The reminder stayed with me through the drive home. When I'd returned to Pine Ridge I thought Samurai Security was behind me. But the unexpected appearance of Blake Weston, and his subsequent murder, had landed the whole mess on my doorstep again, and nearly drawn me back into the world of high tech.

There was still the matter of Samurai's finances to sort out. A small army of lawyers and accountants were trying to untangle the mess. One of these days, they told me, there might be a financial settlement due me.

I wasn't holding my breath.

By the time I hauled the last load of grocery bags into the kitchen, Mom was unpacking the first bags and putting them away. I got another of her raised-eyebrow looks when she opened the refrigerator to put away the salad. She didn't have to say anything—we replayed the same conversation every time she looked in my fridge.

First she would bemoan the state of my nutrition, then she'd move on to how she'd taught me better eating habits, and finally she'd sigh deeply and tell me that soon I would regret not taking better care of myself.

"Just wait until you turn forty, Georgiana—and it's not that far away, you know. You can't eat like this forever." I realized she had been talking for several minutes without me really hearing her.

"I've got a long way till forty," I countered. "And I don't 'eat like this' all the time. I just hadn't been to the grocery store this week."

Well, maybe I hadn't been to the grocery store this month, but I'd been busy. I had my licensing exam coming up soon, and I'd been spending every spare minute studying.

The exam had me spooked. I'd done fine on all the classroom work in my nearly four years in the apprenticeship program, and I had a bachelor's and a master's degree from Caltech—one of the toughest schools in the country. But test anxiety was still an old nemesis. Intense preparation was my main defense, and I wanted to pass this thing the first time.

"And don't tell me how hard you've been studying. That's no excuse. In fact"—she closed the refrigerator and leveled her gaze at me—"you should be more careful of your diet when you're under stress. It's a fact that proper nutrition is essential to proper brain function."

She had me there, though I wasn't about to admit it. And how did she know what I was thinking? It was a mom talent that I thought should have gone away when I was no longer a teenager, but it hadn't.

I pulled a jar of premade spaghetti sauce from a bag

and set it by the stove. Next to it I put a package of spaghetti noodles, some pre-sliced mushrooms, and a small package of Italian sausage.

"Spaghetti sauce from a *jar*?" The disapproval was clear in her voice.

"If we want to eat tonight instead of tomorrow," I explained as I dragged a saucepan from the cupboard, "I have to take some shortcuts."

I dumped the sauce in the pan and put it on to heat, then got a frying pan and threw the sausage in.

Mom puttered around the kitchen, making unnecessary small talk about dinner and fiddling with one thing and another while I cooked and drained the sausage and added it to the bubbling sauce.

We were carefully avoiding the one subject that was foremost on both our minds: the death of Gregory Whitlock.

Finally I couldn't stand it any longer.

"I really am sorry, Mom."

She looked at me. Her expression said she didn't understand what I meant, though I was sure she did. After several seconds she abandoned the attempt, her face crumpling momentarily with grief before she regained her usual iron control.

"You never liked him, Georgie," she said, her voice soft with a vulnerability she never displayed in public. "You must be"—she hesitated as though searching for the right word—"*relieved*."

"No." I shook my head. "I admit, Gregory wasn't one of my favorite people, but this isn't the time or place for that discussion. What's important right now is you. You loved him. I want to be here for whatever you need."

"I've been through this before, Georgiana." Her usual commanding tone was back, the moment of weakness buried once again. "It's not easy, but you do what has to be done."

I wanted to ask her how she did that, how she buried her feelings. But just then the doorbell rang.

"Watch this for me, would you please?" I said, hurrying to the front door.

"I walked them," Sue said as she handed me a shopping bag and unclipped the dogs' leashes. "And they had dinner. Don't listen when they tell you they haven't."

I chuckled. Sue was a sucker for dogs of all kinds, and my two knew that well. "They gave you the sad starving-puppy eyes, didn't they? You are such an easy touch."

I glanced in the bag. Flannel pajamas with subdued stripes. Mom would approve. I gave Sue a brief nod of thanks.

"Hello, Sue," Mom called from the kitchen. "How are you?"

"I'm fine, Mrs. Neverall."

I rolled my eyes. Sue and I had been best friends since we were kids, and even though she could refer to Mom as Sandra when we talked about her, she couldn't bring herself to call her anything but Mrs. Neverall to her face.

In the kitchen, Mom had somehow assumed control in the two minutes I'd been gone. The table was set with napkins carefully folded at each place, the garlic bread was in the oven, and pasta was boiling merrily on the stove.

How did she *do* that?

We made polite small talk for several minutes while Mom finished the bread and pasta and I tossed the bagged salad into a bowl and added a drizzle of Italian dressing.

By the time we sat down to eat, however, we had exhausted all the carefully neutral topics. We served ourselves and began to eat in an increasingly uncomfortable silence.

I didn't know how much longer I could stand it before I said something—*anything*—to break the silence. My brilliant plan to have Sue help me through the first night of Mom's stay wasn't working.

This was worse than I had imagined, and it was only the beginning. I wouldn't last a week.

I waited, hoping Mom would relax a little, would stop pretending there was nothing unusual about her having dinner at my house, or spending the night with me. Nothing unusual about finding her fiancé dead under her house.

Not likely. Sandra Neverall had established the rules and she would expect everyone around her to live by them.

Well, I didn't have to play by her rules. This was my house, my dinner table, and I wasn't going to be shoved back into the role of the dutiful daughter trying—and failing—to please her mother.

"Mom," I said, in what I hoped was a casual tone, "do you know what those boxes are that Gregory had under the house?"

"Boxes?"

"Yeah. There were a bunch of wooden boxes. Shipping crates of some kind. I wondered if you knew what he was storing under there."

Mom shook her head. "He wasn't storing anything under the house."

"So you didn't know they were there?" I countered, twirling pasta around my fork with a nonchalance I didn't feel.

"There wasn't anything to know, Georgiana. Gregory wasn't storing anything under my house."

I chewed for a moment, considering whether to press the issue. Sue shot me a warning look, but my curiosity was aroused.

"Under the hallway, I think." I thought for a minute, trying to picture what I'd seen. But all that would come back was the image of a misshapen lump and a pair of unmoving penny loafers. "I know they were there. I saw them."

I shoved away the thought of the other things I had seen under the house. I didn't want to think about that again. Ever.

Mom shook her head, her expression puzzled. "No, Georgie," she said, slipping back into my childhood nickname. "Gregory has a nice big house of his own. There isn't any reason for him to store anything under my house."

It didn't take a brain trust to see where this was going. Mom truly did not know about the crates under her house. Sandra Neverall could be the Queen of Denial when she wanted to be, but this time she was clearly sincere.

Which meant Gregory had stashed something under there without telling her. And that meant it was something he didn't want her to know about.

But what could he have wanted to hide from her?

And why not keep the crates at his own house?

But saying that to my mother wasn't a good idea.

We finished eating in silence.

chapter 6

Daisy stuck her cold nose against my face, demanding I wake up. I swatted her away and tried to roll over. The alarm hadn't gone off. I didn't need to get up yet.

But instead of the expanse of my queen-size bed, I found my face shoved against the back of the sofa. Something twisted around my waist, defying my efforts to get comfortable, and the sharp aroma of fresh coffee assaulted my sleep-addled brain.

There shouldn't be coffee when I wasn't awake yet. And why had I fallen asleep in my clothes on the couch?

I propped myself up on one elbow, staring blearily around the living room. Something was very wrong here.

The sound of the shower running in the bathroom brought the events of the previous day flooding back.

I was sleeping on the sofa deliberately, wearing brand-new pajamas courtesy of Sue.

And my mother was in my shower.

I groaned and flopped back down on the sofa, bumping my head against the arm. Hard.

I groaned again.

This was never going to work.

Daisy and Buddha stood at the edge of the sofa, looking at me. Their expressions said quite clearly that something wasn't right. They didn't know how to react to someone in their house while I was asleep.

True, Wade had stayed one night following Blake Weston's death, but our relationship hadn't reached the bedroom stage, much less the sleepover stage. He had stayed on the sofa. And Wade was already a part of Daisy and Buddha's pack. My mother wasn't.

I stumbled into the kitchen, where the coffee had finished dripping, and filled a heavy pottery mug from the carafe. Ignoring the pressure in my bladder, I wandered into my workout room and swapped Sue's pajamas for underwear, a plain white T-shirt, and a pair of no-name jeans. A clean pair of coveralls were already in the Beetle with my toolbox and my boots.

The shower stopped.

I waited several minutes, thinking Mom would come out of the bathroom at any moment. I let the dogs outside and watched them while I sipped the cooling mug of coffee. The warmth was comforting, and the caffeine was beginning to kick in.

I hoped Mom would finish up in the bathroom soon. My rental house had exactly one bathroom. I was regretting that fact bitterly right now.

After the dogs came in and had their breakfast, I was beginning to think my mother had taken up permanent residence in there.

Finally I heard the door open, and I hurried toward the hall, anxious to take care of my morning routine. My short brown hair was still uncombed, and I needed to wash my face.

Steam billowed into the hall, smelling of perfumed soap, expensive body lotion, and shampoo. Mom emerged from the cloud of steam wrapped in a heavy terry-cloth robe, the kind upscale hotels will sell to guests at a couple hundred bucks a pop.

I scooted past her in the narrow hallway and shut the bathroom door. I was too desperate to make polite conversation.

If anything, the steam was thicker in the tiny room, the smell of the soap and lotion nearly overwhelming in the enclosed space. I quickly did my business and emerged a few minutes later—along with the remnants of the steam cloud—my hair combed and my teeth brushed, carrying the empty coffee mug and as ready as I was going to be to face the day.

Mom was waiting in the hallway, still in her bathrobe, a cup of coffee in her hand. Her hair was damp and she wore no makeup.

"Is this the only bathroom?" she asked, annoyance creeping into her voice. When I nodded, she shook her head. "I guess I'm used to having my own. Gregory's house has three, after all. We'll have to work out a better schedule for the mornings."

My house, my bathroom—I'm practically dancing in the hallway waiting for her to get through, and *she* thought we needed a better schedule for the morning?

This was never going to work.

Mom was heading for the bathroom door again, and I was sure it would be another long visit, this time involving blow dryers, makeup, and several more mysterious beauty products.

I didn't miss having to do all that. All Barry expected of his crew was to be clean and neat. I'd had my days of high-maintenance hair and wardrobe in San Francisco, and I had happily left it all behind.

"I've gotta go to work, Mom. There's a spare key on the hook by the back door that you can take. Just make sure you lock up when you leave." I waved my empty mug in her direction. "Thanks for making coffee. Call me if you need me."

I dropped the dirty mug in the sink on my way out.

I was still working at the McComb castle, as I had been on and off for over a year. Chad and Astrid McComb were prime examples of the Northwest species known as Microsoft millionaires. Young and brilliant, they had devoted many years to the high-tech firm that called the Northwest home. Their reward for immersing themselves in their careers 24/7 was stock options and profit participation that allowed them to retire in their forties and do almost anything they wanted.

They wanted a castle, and they had the money to make it a reality. The death of Blake Weston in their under-construction moat had tarnished the dream for a while. But now that the moat was finished and the structure was nearing completion, they were eagerly looking forward to moving in.

Sean Jacobs, the crew chief, had given me the job of installing the kitchen fixtures. I considered it a major compliment. It had taken two years of working harder than any man on the crew, but I had gained Sean's respect. For a guy with ex-wife issues, he'd come a long way.

I arrived at the job site before the rest of the crew. I'd always relished those few minutes of peace and quiet before the workday started. When I was running Samurai Security it was my most productive time of day; no interruptions, no phone calls, no meetings and appointments. I accomplished more in the two hours before my employees arrived than I did in the other twelve.

Now I leaned against the fender of the Beetle, sipping a latte from the drive-through and watching the forest around the castle come to life.

Chad and Astrid were building their castle outside the urban growth boundaries. It was the only way they could get permits for turrets and a moat, and even then they had spent almost as much on legal wrangling as they had on construction. But as a result, they were in the middle of several square miles of undeveloped foothills covered with tall evergreens and oak trees.

The sun was bright, and a warm breeze carried the tang of pine needles. Birdsong drifted through the clear morning air, and I watched a couple squirrels chase each other up a tree. I sighed contentedly, savoring the moments of isolation and peace.

Within minutes all of that dissolved into the noise and

bustle of a busy construction site. Pickups growled up the hill carrying workmen, tools, and supplies, their tires crunching in the gravel parking pad at the top.

Sean's truck pulled up next to me. Parking on the castle side of the moat was limited and reserved for heavy loads like fixtures and building materials that were trucked across the main bridge. The crews parked outside and walked across a small footbridge.

"Ready to finish that kitchen?" Sean called over the top of the Beetle.

I nodded and grabbed my toolbox. Time to get to work.

Early in my plumbing career I had realized that plumbers spent a lot of time under sinks or under houses. The kitchen assignment meant I was working under the sink. It was much nicer than crawling under a house.

Especially a house with a body under it.

I shoved aside thoughts of Gregory and focused on the job at hand.

The dishwasher was in place, ready for me to hook up, along with the garbage disposal, and there were three different sinks to connect. I had plenty to keep me occupied.

I started with the hot water supply valve and hose. With the valve in place and the hose tightened onto the valve fitting, I threaded the supply and drain hoses through the opening in the cabinet wall next to the sink.

I had just crawled under the sink and worked myself into position to reach the hoses and connect them when I heard a heavy tread moving across the empty kitchen.

Occasionally the electrical or drywall crews had to interrupt my work as they made changes, and I expected to see a pair of workmen's boots.

Instead I saw a pair of spit-polished black oxfords. No one on a construction site wore a pair of shoes like that—they belonged with a uniform, and I instantly realized who they belonged to. It was my plumber super-power: I recognized people by their shoes.

"Hello, Sheriff," I called from under the sink, without

bothering to look any closer. "Is there something I can do for you?"

I saw the shoes flex and heard the creak of leather as Fred Mitchell crouched down and peered under the sink. "You could come in and make your statement, Miss Neverall."

There was a chuckle in his voice that belied the overly formal address, and although he didn't crack a smile there was a hint of amusement in his eyes.

"Oh, sh-*oot*." I bit back the expletive that had nearly escaped. One of Barry's rules was no foul language on the job. He was probably the only man in the construction trade on the planet that didn't swear a blue streak, but he said it was disrespectful of the clients, so his employees didn't swear on the job. Even when the clients weren't around.

I slid out from under the sink and effortlessly pulled myself into a sitting posture. Amazing what two years of crawling under sinks could do for your abs. "Sorry, Sheriff. I got distracted trying to get my mother settled and I just completely forgot."

I glanced at the cheap plastic watch on my wrist—never wear a good watch when you're working on pipes, a lesson I'd learned the hard way—and calculated how long the current job would take. "If I work through lunch I should be through about one thirty," I offered. "How about if I come by your office before I go home?"

"That will be fine." The sheriff paused, and a look of genuine concern crossed his face. "How is your mother, Georgie? That must have been quite a shock . . ." His voice trailed off, leaving a question hanging in the air.

I couldn't think of a way to really explain that she was being her usual tightly controlled self and I had no real idea how she was beneath the calm façade. "She just found out her fiancé is dead, she's been thrown out of her own house, and her office has to be a complete mess with Gregory's *death*." The word still stuck in my throat, but I was getting used to it. "How do you think she is?"

My tone was sharper than I intended. Clearly the situation was getting to me. I could only imagine how it felt to my mother.

"Sorry," I added. "It's a strain," I said more calmly. "She hasn't talked about it, but I know it's affecting her."

The sheriff shrugged. "I'm going to have to talk to her soon," he said.

"I know." It was my turn to shrug. I waved a hand toward the sink. "Well, I better get back to this, if I'm going to come by the office this afternoon." I turned to crawl back under the sink. "Unless there was something else?"

The sheriff looked as though he wanted to say more, but he just shook his head. His Sam Brown belt creaked as he straightened up. "Go back to work. I'll see you at the office about one thirty."

He hesitated for a few seconds longer before he turned and strode out of the kitchen. I heard him exchange a greeting with one of the painters as he passed through the dining room.

It had been an odd visit. He acted as though he wanted to ask more questions, yet he had really only reminded me to come by the office and make my statement.

I shook my head and went back to work.

I was sure I'd find out soon enough what was on his mind.

chapter 7

I finished early and decided I needed lunch before I faced the sheriff.

A couple quick phone calls and I had company. Sue was ready for a break and Paula Ciccone, Barry's wife and the Pine Ridge librarian, agreed to meet us at Franklin's.

My aging Beetle looked right at home in the parking lot of the Googie-style coffee shop. The expansive front windows and cantilevered concrete roof that typified the style testified to the origin of the building in the early 1960s, when Pine Ridge was a dinner stop on the way home from a day of skiing on Mount Hood.

Inside, Franklin's hadn't changed much in the decades since. The booths lined against the front window were dark vinyl, the walls were covered with fake stone made of concrete, and the stainless-steel kitchen was clearly visible from the swivel stools that lined the counter.

Sue and I settled into a booth where we could watch for Paula. We didn't need to look at the menu. It hadn't changed since we were kids. Good iced tea and the best club sandwich I'd ever had.

Paula arrived a couple minutes later, out of breath.

"The tenth-graders took longer than I expected," she panted, sliding in next to me. "Too busy sizing up date choices to focus on their book choices." She sighed. "As if I didn't get enough of that at home."

I chuckled. Barry and Paula had married young and their youngest daughter had turned fourteen a few months ago. I knew from the stories Barry told that Megan was a greater challenge than both the older girls put together.

Megan was the reason I even had a job with Barry. A couple years earlier she had chided her father about the absence of women on his crew. When I began looking for an apprentice spot Barry was eager to hire a woman, if only to get out of the doghouse with Megan.

"Still battling the raging teenage hormones?" Sue asked with a grin.

Since neither of us had kids, we could tease Paula without fear. My dogs might occasionally misbehave, but it was nothing compared to a rebellious teenager.

Paula shook her head and groaned softly. "My mother tried to warn me. She said 'Never let them outnumber you,' and she was right. But we didn't listen." She shook her head, but it was more a gesture of amusement than denial. It was clear she enjoyed the challenge of Megan, whatever she said.

"Can we talk about something besides my wayward daughter?"

I was still laughing when the waitress appeared to take our order. I paid careful attention to the ordering process ever since the day I'd been so distracted I didn't notice I had egg salad until I bit into it.

I hate egg salad.

"I have to watch my time," I said. "I promised Sue's boyfriend I'd be at his office at one thirty." I threw Sue a glance and continued. "Wouldn't want him tracking me down on the job. Again."

"On the job?" Paula said, her voice rising in indignation.

"Georgie, you know he has to take your statement!" Sue protested.

"What? He can't use a telephone?" Paula wasn't letting this one go.

"He tried! Several times." Sue stopped suddenly. She grabbed her iced tea and sucked on the straw, staring into the glass as though it was the most fascinating thing in the world.

She could avoid looking at us, but she couldn't stop the blush that spread up her neck and covered her face.

"Uh, Sue?" I wished I could cock one eyebrow like everyone else on the planet. This was the perfect time for that expression. "What did he try"—I paused for dramatic effect—"*several* times?"

Beside me Paula gasped, then giggled. Sue turned even redder, if that was possible.

I couldn't keep a straight face.

"Never mind," I said through the giggles that erupted. "I think I know!"

"You two have very dirty minds!"

"Us?" I proclaimed in mock outrage. "You're the one turning several colors of red. What are we supposed to think?"

Sue's color slowly subsided. She waited a moment, then said stubbornly, "Well, he *did* try to call."

That brought a fresh wave of giggles from me and Paula, and finally a lopsided grin from Sue. Her relationship with the sheriff was still new, and we were all trying to figure out where it fit with our friendships. But no matter what, Sue would always be my best friend.

"So what's the problem?" Paula said. "Why is 'Fred,'"— she made the quotation marks with her fingers—"so intent on talking to you?"

It was our turn to stare at her.

"You don't know?" I managed at last.

"Know what?"

"About Gregory Whitlock," Sue said.

Paula shook her head. "I know that. Everyone in town knows. But just because Georgie got herself involved in a couple murders . . ." Her voice trailed off and she reached up to touch the brooch she wore on her jacket.

I don't think Paula even realized she was fingering Martha Tepper's brooch, the one that had drawn me into the mystery of Miss Tepper's disappearance and led to the discovery of her murder.

Sue's eyes widened. "Then you don't know!"

"Know what?" Paula's voice rose, and her hand dropped back to the table. The spoon rattled in my iced tea glass. "How could I know what you're talking about when you're talking in circles?"

There was a flash of the infamous Ciccone temper Barry talked about.

"Paula."

She turned to look at me.

"You heard he was dead, right?"

She nodded.

"Did you hear where he was found?"

She furrowed her brow for a moment. "He wasn't at home," she said slowly, thinking aloud. "Something about someone else's house." She thought for a minute longer, then shook her head. "No, I think that's all I heard."

I took a deep breath. "It was my mother's house," I said. I fought back the panic that tried to overwhelm me every time I thought about it. "He was under the house."

I could see the understanding begin to dawn in her expression.

I nodded. "I found him."

"Oh, Georgie!" She threw her arm over my shoulders and gave me an awkward, one-armed hug. "How awful for you!"

I tried to shrug off her concern, unwilling to face the harsh reality of what I'd seen. "Worse for my mother."

"Of course! How is she, Georgie? Is there anything I can do?"

Sue's bark of harsh laughter drew Paula's attention.

"She's doing her usual thing," I said, and Paula looked back at me. "Claims she's fine, that she doesn't need anything. I'll bet she's at the office right now, trying to act like it's business as usual." I shook my head. "That's my mother."

"Tell her the worst part," Sue said.

"There's more?" Paula sounded incredulous. After all, when your mother's fiancé is dead, and you found the body, how much worse can it be?

"She's staying with me."

Paula winced and gave my shoulder another squeeze before she moved her arm. "Okay," she agreed, "that's worse."

"I don't know how long I can do this. She's already taken over the bathroom, and I think the kitchen is next."

"That would be an improvement," Sue said, then looked sheepish. "I mean, your mom's a good cook, Georgie. You said so yourself."

"I manage," I muttered. I'd known how to cook once upon a time. My mother had insisted that a woman needed to know how to prepare a proper meal. But when you work through dinner, you get used to takeout or ordering in and actual cooking goes by the wayside.

"Never mind," Paula said in her best everybody-play-nice voice. "What can we do to help, Georgie?"

"Nothing. That's the worst part. Right now I can't do anything. The only thing we can do is hold on until the sheriff lets Mom back into her house." I glanced at my watch. "And speaking of our esteemed sheriff, I am going to have to run. Don't want to be late."

Sue made a face, but she didn't say anything. I dropped some bills on the tabletop as Paula moved to let me out. "Call me later," she said. "Just let me know you're okay."

Sue reached out and touched my arm. "Me, too," she said.

I nodded to both of them and headed for the car.

chapter 8

I parked in the sheriff's lot with a couple minutes to spare. By the time I locked up the Beetle—force of habit, who'd be stupid enough to steal an old Beetle from a sheriff's office parking lot?—I was right on time to meet Sheriff Mitchell.

Mitchell was waiting in the now-familiar interrogation room. At least he didn't keep me waiting as he had on past visits. I wasn't sure whether I should be relieved or suspicious. I settled on wait-and-see.

"Thank you for coming." The sheriff gestured to the chair across from him. I'd grown used to the battered steel-and-cracked-vinyl side chair. I was surprised to see something a little newer in its place.

Newer was a relative term I realized as I sat down. This one might have a little more padding, though it wasn't a vast improvement. Still, it seemed like the sheriff was making an effort.

Once I was settled, the sheriff took out his pocket recorder. I was used to this part, too. He always claimed it was so he could be sure he remembered things correctly. Not that I believed him.

"You mind?" he asked.

I could have objected but what was the point? I was there to give a statement, and we'd done this dance before.

"Go right ahead."

He switched on the recorder, set it to voice activation, and tested it by giving the date and time. When he was satisfied it was working properly he sat back a few inches and leveled his gaze at me.

"You're developing a bad habit of finding dead bodies, Miss Neverall."

I shrugged. "It's not exactly my fault, Sheriff. I'm certainly not the one responsible for them."

He sighed. "I suppose not. But this is the third time you've done this. Tell me, Georgie, did you have this knack for finding bodies when you lived in San Francisco, or is it something special about Pine Ridge?"

I can recognize a rhetorical question when I hear it. I kept my mouth shut.

"How well did you know Mr. Whitlock?"

I thought about the question. I'd tried to be cordial to Gregory for my mother's sake, but I had to admit I hadn't known much about him. "He and my mother worked together. I think they started dating before I moved back to Pine Ridge, but I wouldn't swear to it. He seemed to be successful. Drove a new car, just built a big new house, got involved with local politics—all the stuff a successful local guy does.

"Beyond that I really didn't know him very well. I had dinner with him and Mom about once a month or so, maybe a little more often since the engagement because there were wedding plans and stuff."

I shoved a strand of hair out of my eyes, the distraction reminding me I needed to get a haircut. "Other than that, I really didn't know much about him."

"You never talked about where he was from, or where he went to school? His hobbies?"

I shook my head.

"Dinner about once a month for a couple years, and you never talked about anything like that?"

I shook my head again. "We didn't have much in common. Mostly we talked about the local sports teams—the high school, or the Blazers—and whether City Hall should be painted this year. You know, the kind of small talk you make when you're being polite."

The sheriff leaned back in his chair and rested his chin on one fist. He rocked slightly as though he was thinking so hard he didn't realize he was moving.

He leaned forward and placed his forearms on the desk. "You didn't like him very much, did you?"

I bristled. "Is that an accusation, Sheriff?"

"No," he said mildly. "But you've already answered my question. You didn't like him." It wasn't a question; it was a statement.

He was right, of course.

I'd tried. I really tried. But there was something about Gregory Whitlock that I had never warmed up to.

A realization hit me, turning the flash of anger to icy cold. "You haven't said anything about how he died, Sheriff. What was it?"

I waited, dread seeping through me. Even before I asked the question I was sure what the answer would be. And I knew I wouldn't like it.

"We're treating his death as a homicide, Miss Neverall." The sheriff retreated into his formal mode again.

Not the answer I wanted.

The sheriff gave me a moment to digest the news, but it was going to take a lot longer than that, even though I was expecting it.

"When did you arrive at your mother's house?"

The sheriff's question drew me back to the events of the previous day. I forced my thoughts back to that morning and tried to remember exactly what I'd done.

"I was at the McComb site in the morning," I said. "Barry and Sean agreed I could inspect Mom's house at lunch, so I left a little early—maybe eleven fifteen or so— and swung by my house to let the dogs out. Figure about fifteen minutes' driving time?"

The sheriff nodded.

I thought for a minute and went on. "I was probably at

home fifteen or twenty minutes, tops. Another five minutes to Mom's house, so I got there just before noon, I'd guess."

"Was there anyone else there when you arrived?"

"Mom was gone, taking some stuff to Gregory's house before she went to the office for the afternoon." I guess Gregory had been there, but I pushed that thought aside.

"And what did you do then?"

"I let myself in the front door. I suppose I didn't even need to go in the house, but I've always had a key and it just seemed like the normal thing to do. I went through the kitchen to the back door—" I stopped, remembering something odd. "I was going to get a drink of water, and I noticed an empty glass on the counter by the sink, which was weird."

Sheriff Mitchell cocked his head to the side. "Why is that weird? You should see the stack of dirty dishes next to my sink." He tried to laugh at his own joke, but it sounded forced.

"Sure, that's normal for most people, but not for Sandra Neverall. You saw her house. There is never, ever, anything out of place. If there's a dirty plate or cup or glass it goes in the dishwasher immediately. She would never leave a dirty glass on the counter."

"Maybe," the sheriff said, but it was clear he wasn't convinced. "So did you get your drink?"

"Yeah. I got a glass of water, then I put both glasses in the dishwasher. Old habits are hard to break. Then I went out the back door and started checking under the house."

"About how long had you been at the house at that point?"

I shrugged. "I don't really know. Maybe eight or ten minutes, I'd imagine. Certainly not much more than that. I didn't go anywhere but the kitchen, and I didn't do anything but get a drink and put the glasses in the dishwasher. It might even have been a couple minutes less than that."

My neck and shoulders tensed, the muscles tightening with stress as the sheriff's questions drew me nearer to the moment I found Gregory.

"Take it easy," the sheriff said as though he could read my mind. "I know this is upsetting, but we'll take it slow. Okay?"

I nodded. Sheriff Mitchell and I weren't always best pals, but it seemed clear he was trying to be considerate and I appreciated the effort.

"Okay. You went out the back door just a few minutes after you arrived at the house. You were getting ready to go under the house. How long before you actually went into the crawl space?"

"Only a minute or two. I checked my flashlight and kind of peered under there, and then I put on my mask and went in."

"You put on a mask?"

"Yeah. It was musty smelling. I thought there might be mold. That's pretty normal."

The sheriff didn't ask any more questions, so I swallowed hard and went on. I told him everything I could remember until I got up to the hard part. I was telling the sheriff about how I'd switched my flashlight back on after noticing the pile of boxes and something else.

I stopped. Several years of martial-arts training had helped me gain some control of my temper, to find the calm inside me. I used the same techniques to help control the panic that threatened to overtake me now.

I closed my eyes for a minute and focused on breathing deep and slow, letting the tension go. It helped a little.

"That 'something else' was Gregory Whitlock?"

"Yes. I got close enough to see what it was and I reached out with my flashlight and kind of tapped it against his foot. He didn't move.

"I got out of there as fast as I could and called 9-1-1. You know the rest."

chapter 9

"How about a break?"

Without waiting for an answer, Sheriff Mitchell stood up. He wiggled his shoulders a little as though trying to release some tension of his own.

At that moment his suggestion made Sheriff Mitchell my best friend. I stood up myself and stretched my arms out, pulling the knots out of my back and shoulders.

The sheriff opened the door to the corridor and spoke to someone outside. I couldn't make out his words, but a minute later a deputy appeared at the door with two cups of coffee.

The sheriff handed one cup to me and carried his around the desk. He resumed his seat, and looked pointedly at the other chair.

I took the hint.

"Just a few more questions," the sheriff tried to reassure me. I hoped he meant it. I was way past ready to be out of there and thinking about anything but the death—the murder—of Gregory Whitlock.

I took a sip of the coffee. It had been sitting too long on the heat, the bitterness of cheap beans burned into the brew.

"You mentioned your mother and Mr. Whitlock's wedding plans a few minutes ago. How was that going?"

Without thinking I rolled my eyes, and the sheriff chuckled.

I realized what I'd done an instant too late. "No, nothing wrong. Just Mom wanting things a certain way. And there was so much to do! She was obsessing over every detail.

"But she just wanted everything to be done right, that's all."

"And you didn't agree?"

"Let's just say Mom and I have different standards about some things."

The sheriff switched tracks. "And how did Mr. Whitlock feel about the wedding preparations? You say you talked with the two of them about the plans. Did he express an opinion?"

I shook my head. "He pretty much stayed out of it. Mom was in charge of the wedding, and Gregory let her do whatever she wanted."

The sheriff sat back in his chair and thought for a long time before he asked his next question. I tried not to fidget, but the chair was putting my butt to sleep.

"You're absolutely sure?" he asked. "There was no question that they were going ahead with the marriage?"

I stared at the sheriff.

I opened my mouth to answer his insane question, but I was at a loss for words. Of all the crazy things I had heard in the last twenty-four hours, this was surely the craziest.

"Okay, I don't know where you got that idea, but the marriage was definitely going to happen. I even witnessed the prenuptial agreement. Not that I really wanted to know all the details of their financial arrangements." I sat back and crossed my arms over my chest. This was one thing I was certain about. "No way either one of them was backing out."

The recorder clicked off when I stopped talking. The constant clicking as it started and stopped was making me nuts, the chair was killing my butt, and the bitter coffee was roiling around in my stomach with my hasty lunch from Franklin's.

"Are we through?" I asked.

Sheriff Mitchell hesitated. He nodded his head. "For now. But I do need to talk to your mother. And"—he gave me a stern look, his eyebrows drawing together over his sharp nose—"you will need to wait and sign your statement after we have it printed.

"You seem to forget about coming back for that little detail."

"Come on, Sheriff. I forgot once. Okay, maybe twice. I'll come in and sign the statement this time. I promise." I looked around for a clock and realized the room didn't have one. Funny, I had never noticed that before.

"As for my mother, she's probably at work this afternoon—"

"No, she isn't," the sheriff interrupted. "The office is closed until we have had time to search Mr. Whitlock's files. No one is allowed in, and no paperwork goes out."

Which meant Mother was probably at my house right this minute, doing Lord knows what.

I had to get back while I could still recognize the place.

It took me several more minutes to convince the sheriff to let me go.

I had to promise not to leave town without letting him know, since I hadn't signed my statement—the guy was never going to get over that flight I took to San Francisco—and we agreed that he would come by the house later to talk to my mother rather than making her come to the station.

I wasn't looking forward to his visit, but at least he would be the one to tell Mom that Gregory's death was being treated as a homicide. She could answer his questions about her wedding plans, if he didn't believe me.

Whatever it took to get me out of the sheriff's station.

Driving away I was torn between going home to rescue my house and my dogs from Mom and stopping to talk to Sue. I was still debating when I passed Doggy Day Spa.

There was an empty parking space at the curb in front and I decided it was a sign I should stop. I wasn't avoiding my mother. Really.

Sue was with a customer when I walked in the store. I waved at her and went through the shop to the office in the back. I could run a computer security scan while I waited for her.

I sat down in front of her computer and started through the familiar routine.

I was still trying to figure out how I felt about walking away from high tech. Blake Weston's death had drawn me back into that world, and for a few crazy days I had seriously considered the offer to return to Samurai Security.

In the end I'd said no.

It wasn't because I didn't like the work. In fact I was enjoying my secret job as a computer consultant and I could have a lot more work if more people knew about my skills and experience.

Which I wasn't sure I wanted. I liked that I only worked for a few close friends, like Sue and Paula and Barry. My computer skills had been a bonus for Barry when he hired me, and I liked making his office computer jump through hoops he didn't know existed.

But the constant pressure and the long hours? No time for a personal life? Devoting every waking hour to the company?

That was the part I didn't miss.

I also didn't miss the rigid schedule of hair and nail appointments to maintain the perfect image of success. I didn't miss being so work-obsessed I had to hire a dog-walker because I didn't have time for Daisy and Buddha. I didn't miss turning every meal into a business meeting and every business meeting into a substitute for real friendships.

Still, I had to admit I missed the money. Living on my wages as an apprentice plumber was a far cry from an income that let me drive a vintage Corvette on the few days I actually had time to drive anywhere.

Now I drove the Beetle my dad had given me when I graduated from high school and I walked my own dogs. I hadn't had a manicure in years, and I trimmed my own hair. I still had the 'Vette though. A woman has to have at least one luxury.

I heard the bell over the front door ring, and a moment later Sue appeared in the door of the office. She ignored the computer screen and pulled a bottle of water from the tiny refrigerator.

"Afraid to go home?" she asked.

"Just stopped to let you know how it went." I sidestepped answering her question.

"And?"

I drew in a deep breath. "Have you heard anything about Gregory and my mom? Anything about problems over the wedding?"

Sue pulled a chair over and sat down. She reached for my hand where it rested on the computer mouse. Her fingers were damp and cold from the water bottle, but the touch was reassuring. "You know I would have told you if I heard anything important," she said. I could hear the *but* in her tone.

"What did you hear that *wasn't* important?"

She sat back and took a long draw on her water bottle. "Nothing, really." She shrugged. "You know how rumors fly in a small town."

"Yeaah." I drew the word out, not sure I wanted to hear the rest.

"Well, I heard they had an argument the other day. In Dee's. Not like a big battle or anything, but it was clear they were disagreeing about something." She shook her head. "You know how it is. I didn't even remember hearing about it until you asked just now."

I groaned. "So that was what he was talking about." I slammed my fist on the desk, making the mouse jump. The cursor skittered across the computer screen, interrupting my scan.

I instantly regretted the flash of temper.

I slowly and deliberately restarted the scan, then moved away from the computer.

Sue watched me without moving. She'd seen me lose it when we were in high school and she still didn't completely trust the new and improved Georgiana Neverall.

"Your boyfriend asked me if there was a problem about the wedding. I had dinner with them a couple days ago. They were getting along just fine." I shook my head, remembering the too-cute antics of my mother fussing over Gregory, and him loving every minute of it. I gave myself a shake to dislodge the image. "So if they had an argument they were definitely over it by the time I saw them."

"That's what I thought, too. I don't know where the rumor started, but somebody said they overheard them arguing about wedding expenses."

I glanced at the computer to check on the progress of the scan. A couple more minutes.

"Fred's only doing his job, Georgie. He has to ask. You know that."

"I suppose." I didn't concede the point with much grace.

Sue looked miserable. I had to admit she was in a tough spot, torn between the man she was dating and her best friend, and I wasn't making it any easier.

"Sorry," I said. I held my right hand up and raised three fingers in a pledge. "I promise not to let issues with boyfriends come between me and my best friend."

Sue laughed. "And vice versa."

I laughed, too. It was an old joke.

"You didn't have to break up with Wade, you know."

"Yes, I did," I insisted. "He shouldn't have covered for that two-timing jerk you were dating. I totally had to."

"Well," she said, standing up and heading back into the shop, "you didn't need to wait twenty years to make up."

"More like fifteen," I said, following her. It probably was closer to twenty than fifteen, but I didn't want to think about how long ago it really was. "And most of that time I wasn't even living here, so it shouldn't count."

"Whatever." Sue dismissed my argument with a wave of her hand. "Seriously, though." She turned around and faced me. "Has anyone told your mother about Gregory?"

She gave me "the look."

"You mean that Fred thinks he was murdered?" The word felt funny on my tongue, but I was getting used to it. I wasn't sure that was a good thing.

"I got the distinct impression the sheriff wants to tell her himself. I may be chicken, but I'm happy to let him."

I looked up at the vintage cat clock on Sue's wall. "And now I had better get going. Even if the sheriff is taking responsibility for talking to her, I think it would be better if I was there.

"Just in case."

chapter 10

The Escalade took up two-thirds of the driveway, and there was a strange car in front of my house when I arrived. I carefully maneuvered the Beetle into the remaining sliver of driveway and locked the doors.

I opened the front door and stepped into chaos.

It appeared to radiate from my mother who stood in the middle of the living room, her hands on her hips, a frown drawing her perfectly arched brows down over her nose.

"No, no, no, Penny. I think the sofa should go over *there*." She waved a gloved hand toward the front wall. "Then we can move the lamp table to the corner—" She stopped when she caught sight of me.

"You remember Penny, don't you, Georgie?" She indicated the young woman who was struggling with the over-stuffed sofa that was my temporary bed. She looked vaguely familiar, like the younger sister of someone I'd gone to school with. Mom didn't bother to fill in the blanks.

"We use her at the agency to clean and stage houses. Since we couldn't meet at the office today"—her tone implied I was somehow to blame for her inconvenience—"I asked her to come here. We finished our business, and then we just sort of . . ." She spread her arms wide, taking in the entire living room. "We won't be long," she said, oblivious to my frozen smile.

Penny caught the look, and there was a flicker of sympathy in her eyes.

"Hi, Penny," I said in what I hoped was a friendly manner. It wasn't her fault my mother was unable to leave my things alone.

Daisy and Buddha appeared in the kitchen doorway, identical expressions of doggy panic on their faces. These strange women were moving furniture in their house while I wasn't there, and they were distressed.

"Mother," I managed to get out through clenched teeth, "can I talk to you for a minute?"

Without waiting for an answer, I walked into the kitchen.

I leaned my back against the counter and crossed my arms over my chest. While I waited for her to join me, I looked around my kitchen.

It wasn't my kitchen anymore. The formerly bare counters now held an assortment of my small appliances that had been stowed in the pantry closet. Each one had been scrubbed and polished, and several dish towels hung from strategic points around the room.

The table, a space usually kept clear, had been covered with a cloth, placemats, a decorative bowl, and a vase of fresh flowers I suspected came from the supermarket.

Which meant Mom had gone grocery shopping, too.

I was still taking in the changes when Mom strode in. Her usual mile-high stilettos had been replaced with a pair of expensive espadrilles, and I was shocked at the realization she was actually several inches shorter than I was.

Even doing housework she had on full makeup, her hair was carefully tied into a loose knot, and she wore a casually stylish outfit of Capri pants and a matching long-sleeved top.

With an expertise born of necessity—dressing for success had taken practice—I could assess her clothes at a glance and I knew her casual outfit was worth more than my entire stock of jeans and T-shirts.

Not that it mattered to me, but I knew it did to her.

"Mom, the sheriff wants to talk to you. He's agreed to

come here rather than make you go to the station, but he'll be here any minute."

"Okay," she said. She looked around the kitchen and glanced back through the door into the living room. Her eyes lit on the dogs, and they moved away from her, as though afraid she was going to banish them from the house.

"I'll just have Penny finish up in the living room while I clean up and change," she went on.

"I doubt there will be time for that," I countered. "You will have to leave the furniture moving for another day." My voice was low, a too-calm tone that most people around me had learned was a warning of the possible release of my tightly controlled anger.

Mom either didn't hear or didn't heed the warning. "It won't take long."

"Mother."

"Yes, dear? What is it?" A note of annoyance crept in, and she looked impatient. "I have to go change."

"Forget changing your clothes and listen to me!" I swallowed the flash of anger and went on. "There isn't time. We need to put the living room back together as best we can and let Penny go home.

"Besides, do you realize you just put my bed directly under the living room window?"

"Don't worry about that, dear. I'm sure the sheriff will get this all straightened out, and I'll be going home in another day or so." She cocked her head to one side in a coquettish gesture meant to indicate she was thinking. "In fact, I'll bet that's why he's coming over."

She sailed back toward the living room, confident that everything would work out.

I admit I took the coward's way out and let her go.

Sure, I could have stopped her and explained that the sheriff was most definitely not coming over to tell her she could go back to her house. But that would have led to questions about why and how I could be so sure. Questions I didn't want to answer.

I followed her into the living room and volunteered to move furniture.

Penny left a few minutes later. Mom followed her to the door, assuring her they would be "back to normal" in a day or two.

She had no idea how wrong she was, nor how fervently I wished she was right. But as Penny pulled away, the sheriff glided into the empty space at the curb. She would know soon.

Fred Mitchell parked his personal pickup and made his way up the walk to the front door. I didn't know why he wasn't driving an official car, but I was just as glad not to have a sheriff's squad car in front of my house.

The sheriff looked exhausted. There were dark circles under his eyes, his usual ramrod-straight posture was sagging slightly, and his uniform was wrinkled, as though he'd slept in it.

Which he probably had.

He had the murder of a prominent local businessman on his hands. I doubted he'd been home since the initial call came in yesterday morning.

I felt sorry for him. After everything else, the next several minutes with my mother would be grueling. And unless he had personally killed Gregory Whitlock—a ludicrous thought—none of it was his fault.

It *was* just his job—a job I didn't envy. I didn't much like talking to him in an official capacity. Would anyone? But when I wasn't the one butting heads with him I realized what a tough position he was in. He had to deal with people at their worst. And my mother's worst? Like I said, I felt sorry for him.

I took the sheriff's jacket and hung it on the coat rack by the front door. "I'd offer you a beer," I said, "but there's that whole 'on duty' thing. How about a cup of coffee?"

He shook his head. "I've had too much already." He winced and instinctively put a hand against his stomach.

"Water?" I suggested.

He nodded.

I went to the kitchen and filled a pitcher. I brought it back to the living room with a couple glasses of ice, just as my mother emerged from the hallway that led to the bedrooms. Somehow in the few intervening minutes she had managed to ditch her casual outfit and replace it with a pair of tailored slacks and a creamy yellow sweater set.

And stilettos.

I managed to keep a straight face. "If you don't need me?" I asked the sheriff, glancing toward the kitchen.

He shook his head. I would be close enough if he wanted me, but I'd leave the two of them alone.

Coward.

I retreated to the kitchen.

I opened the refrigerator, intending to make dinner. I confronted full shelves, a novelty in my kitchen, and a couple plates already filled and covered with plastic wrap, ready to microwave and serve.

My mother needed a hobby. Or at least to get back to work.

I set my laptop on the kitchen table and flipped it open. Maybe I could distract myself by checking my e-mail or cruising the Web. Anything to take my mind off the interview taking place a few feet away.

There was an open doorway between the two rooms, so I could hear them talking. I couldn't make out all the words at first, but as I grew accustomed to the sound of their voices I could make out most of the conversation.

It wasn't eavesdropping as much as hearing a conversation I couldn't avoid.

"I hope you don't mind," the sheriff said.

I felt a smile curl my mouth. I could picture him taking out the little recorder and putting it on the table next to the water pitcher.

"It's just for my own use. Make sure I remember everything correctly."

"Of course," Mom answered.

The sheriff went through his ritual, a process that had

become all too familiar to me over the last couple years. It was all new to my mother.

I logged in to the laptop and brought up the mail program. I didn't need to listen; I knew what was coming.

I deleted several messages from my junk folder offering to check my credit score, enlarge body parts, or find long-lost schoolmates, and reset my spam filters. It was the kind of work I could do without much thought, a good idea since I couldn't completely tune out the voices in the living room.

I managed pretty well though, until my mother's voice rose. "Sheriff. You must be mistaken! That simply isn't possible."

Mom didn't sound upset so much as she sounded offended. It was the same tone she had taken with Sheriff Mitchell when he questioned me as a possible suspect in the murder of Blake Weston, an implication that her boyfriend— or her daughter—simply couldn't be involved with something as unseemly as murder.

While I didn't share her absolute belief in Gregory, I did share her desire not to be involved. Not that it mattered what we wanted. Blake Weston's death had made that clear. When someone you're close to—or someone you used to be close to—is murdered, you're involved whether you want to be or not.

The sheriff spoke softly, offering his apologies for the questions he had to ask, while pressing ahead with his interview.

He asked about her relationship with Gregory, which she insisted was happy. She told him there was no problem with the wedding plans, and that she was already moving into the new house Gregory had purchased.

"This house—" I heard him riffle through the pages of the small notebook he carried as a backup to the recorder. "You say Mr. Whitlock *built* it?"

"He had a mortgage, of course," Mom answered. "But yes, he built it."

"And did you have a financial interest in the property?"

Mom didn't answer immediately. The sudden silence drew my full attention, and I sat still, listening.

She laughed, as though trying to dismiss the question. "I did cover part of the down payment and closing costs," she admitted. "And I certainly expected to pay my share of the expenses. I hardly expected Gregory to support me. I'm perfectly capable of supporting myself."

That was a change that had come about in the five years since my father's death, and Mom had become fiercely proud of it.

"And the incident at Dee's?"

"Incident? You mean that little disagreement?" I heard the pitcher clink against the table and the sound of pouring water. "It was just a misunderstanding, Sheriff. More embarrassing than anything. I would have preferred we have the discussion in private, but Gregory was insistent we resolve the issue while we ate breakfast.

"It was over in a few minutes. The rather public nature of the conversation made me lose my appetite."

Ah, yes. Never argue in public. One of Mother's rules.

The conversation continued on that track for several minutes and I went back to my computer. I hadn't heard anything I didn't already know.

Even the part about the down payment on the house had been spelled out in the prenuptial agreement, and Mom had insisted I read every word.

"I don't know anything about boxes!" Mom raised her voice, and my attention was drawn back to the living room. "I didn't know they were there. I don't know what was in them, and I don't know when or why they were put there. And I only have your word that they belonged to Gregory. For all I know, they could have been anyone's."

"They were addressed to Mr. Whitlock at his home," the sheriff said. His voice was patient, but I could hear the strain. Talking to my mother was often difficult under the best of circumstances. Which this definitely wasn't.

"Do you know what was in them?" Mom challenged.

"The way this works, Mrs. Neverall, is that *I* ask the questions and *you* answer them. Not the other way around."

"If they were under my house, Sheriff, no one told me."

"Who has access to your house, Mrs. Neverall?"

"My housekeeper, Penny. My daughter—and you can't possibly suspect her. Again." Sarcasm dripped from the last word. She still hadn't forgiven the sheriff for suspecting me in Blake's death.

"Anyone else?"

"Gregory, of course." She paused. "No one else."

"Did anyone lose a key? Or would any of those people lend their key to someone else? Is there any way someone other than those three would have access to your house?"

Mom sighed. "No, Sheriff. No one else. I doubt Georgie has used her key at all since she's been back, except for her visit to check the pipes."

"And the housekeeper?"

"She wouldn't let that key out of her sight if she cares about her job. Which, I have to say, she does. I pay her well, Sheriff. You must always respect the people you allow to care for your home."

The implication of her words finally sank in. My mother had a housekeeper! The woman who nagged and sniffed at my lack of domestic skills *paid* someone to clean for her.

A grin spread across my face as I realized the leverage she had just provided me. No more looking down her nose at my dusty bookshelves and jumbled closets. No more snide remarks about the dog hair in the carpet.

"So what was in those boxes, Sheriff?"

"Wine," the sheriff replied. He waited for a response from my mother and when he didn't get one he continued, "It seems odd, don't you think, that Mr. Whitlock would put several cases of wine under your house when he had a very nice wine cellar in your new house?"

"I have no idea, Sheriff. Perhaps he put it there before we finished the new house and he hadn't had time to move it yet. Maybe it was a surprise for our wedding. I really can't even guess as to why he did something I didn't know about."

"But you did know about the wine cellar, didn't you? Did you know Mr. Whitlock was amassing a large wine collection?"

"Of course I knew there was a wine cellar. As for Gregory's wine collection, as you call it, he had been buying wine for a long while. I'd hardly call it a collection."

Mom's voice strained just as mine had earlier in the day. "Are we through here?"

She got the same hesitation and eventual answer I had.

The sheriff agreed they were through for the night, but he warned her he would have more questions, and she would need to sign a statement.

And he told her not to leave town.

He was adamant about that last part.

Make sure you rotate the handles on your plumbing shut-off valves twice a year. The valves to your toilets, to your sinks, to your house, to your washing machine, to your dishwasher and so on—all of them can degrade and seize up if they aren't turned regularly. You'll spot any issues early, if there are any, and prevent most problems from happening in the first place. Turn the valves off and on when you change your batteries for your smoke detectors. I do this when daylight saving time starts and stops. It makes the semiannual task easy to schedule and remember. This small precaution means that when you really need to turn off one of these valves in an emergency, you'll know where to find it, and it will be in working order. If you don't know where these valves are, ask your plumber to show you the next time he visits your home.

—A Plumber's Tip from Georgiana Neverall

chapter 11

I stayed in the kitchen until Mom closed the front door behind the sheriff and I heard his car pull away from the curb.

Sheriff Mitchell had a point. It did seem odd that Gregory would put wine under Mom's house when there was a wine cellar in his new house. Especially wine that he'd bothered to have shipped from Europe to his new home. You didn't pay international shipping for a thirty-dollar Bordeaux or Pinot Noir.

And there had been several cases of wine.

What had he been up to?

I was about to start a Web search for information on expensive wine, when Mom stomped into the kitchen, her stiletto heels beating an angry tattoo against the aged linoleum on my floor.

She pulled the dinner plates from the refrigerator, along with a bowl of salad and a small jar of homemade dressing. For a fleeting moment I was impressed by her preparations, but my awe was quickly replaced by amusement. I knew her secret now.

She had a housekeeper.

Made it a lot easier to look like a domestic goddess when someone else did the mundane work.

"Dinner's almost ready," she said, swapping plates in the microwave. "You need to go wash up."

I shut the laptop and went, as if I were ten years old again.

Dinner was a strained affair. She didn't bring up her interview with the sheriff, and I didn't ask. I didn't want to admit I had overheard most of their conversation, although I was sure she knew I had.

I told her about the progress on the McComb job, and she nodded and made appropriate polite noises, just as though she gave a flying fig.

We were clearing the table when she stretched elaborately and covered a yawn with her hand. The diamond in her engagement ring flashed, and I worked at not noticing that she was still wearing Gregory's ring.

"I think I'll take a bath and turn in early," she said.

"Just let me in there a minute, and it's all yours," I answered. At least for one day the morning bathroom traffic jam would be averted, if I showered tonight.

The dishwasher was loaded and the table wiped down when I returned. Mom gave me a little hug and disappeared into the bathroom, leaving me alone with the rest of the evening in front of me.

I was still dressed, it was early, and I caught myself pacing around the kitchen like a caged animal. Daisy and Buddha seemed to pick up on my tension, padding from their beds to the kitchen and back.

I scribbled a note to my mother, telling her I was going to walk the dogs. She'd worry no matter what, but at least I tried. I left the note in the middle of the bare kitchen table, where she couldn't miss it.

"Come on, guys," I said, heading for the front door. "Let's get out of here for a while."

I grabbed the leashes and clipped them to their collars. Just walking the dogs. That was all I was up to.

Once outside I glanced over at the Beetle snuggled up against Mom's Escalade. We might be moving soon, after all, and it couldn't hurt to let the dogs explore their new neighborhood, could it? It was just a get-acquainted walk in the place where we might be living.

Daisy and Buddha were always up for a car ride, and they piled enthusiastically into the back of the Beetle. It had taken me a long time to convince them dogs ride in back, but they had finally stopped trying to sneak into the passenger seat.

Most of the time.

"Daisy," I said warningly. She looked up at me, the picture of innocence, from her perch in the front seat. Her expression was one of befuddlement, which I totally did not believe. "Backseat!" I ordered.

With a big doggy sigh, she threaded her way between the front seats and settled into the back.

I parked around the corner from Mom's house and let the dogs out. I headed away from the house, as though to reinforce the argument that I was just exploring the neighborhood.

We circled around a couple blocks, the dogs stopping every few feet to sniff a strange bush or mark a tree. This was their new territory and I gave them plenty of time to acquaint themselves with it.

I needed the time to orient myself, too. I had lived here when I was in high school, but that was several years ago. It was full dark, with lights burning in the windows of houses set well back from the edge of the road.

I stayed on the roadway, not trusting the shoulder in the blackness. Eventually I would learn, but for tonight this was unexplored territory.

We turned another corner and I could see Mom's house in the next block. Well, I could see the one house with no lights, a dark hulk against the darker night. It wasn't a comforting sight.

Between here and there was Harry Hamilton's place. Harry was the quintessential neighborhood gossip. He seemed to spend most of his days, and evenings, drinking coffee in the living room with the drapes wide open to a view of all the houses on the block. If anything happened on this street the odds were Harry had seen it. Harry was the one who'd called my mother the day Gregory was killed.

I crossed the street in case Harry was watching, thankful for the dark. It was a public road, and I had every right to be there, but I didn't like being watched. It was something I should have thought about before I agreed to buy the house. I was going to have Harry Hamilton for a neighbor.

I glanced over at Harry's place as we hurried past, a sigh of relief escaping my lips at the sight of closed drapes.

We crossed the side street passing under the lone street light on the block and approached the dark spot that was Mom's house.

On the other side of the street a blue glow in the Gordens' living room showed they were watching TV. A faint light came on in their kitchen window and I could imagine Mr. Gorden opening the refrigerator for his nightly beer. It was a ritual he'd observed since I was a grade school kid doing homework at the kitchen table with his daughter, Melissa. Melissa had moved to Colorado several years ago according to my mother, but the Gordens sill lived in the same house and kept to the same schedule they'd always had.

Next door, Mrs. Sweeney's kitchen window was dark. She hadn't lived next door to Mom for very long, and I didn't know much about her.

No one took any notice of me.

I passed the house and continued to the end of the block before turning around and coming back. I watched the other houses for any sign that someone was interested in what I was doing, but I didn't see anything.

My heart sped up as I drew closer to the driveway. No one guarded the house, and the only sign that it was a crime scene was a couple strands of yellow tape hanging from the hinges of the back gate.

The sheriff had told Mom not to go back inside until they were done, but he hadn't told me I couldn't go in. For that matter, the front door wasn't even marked with crime-scene tape. Not that I intended to go inside, but it couldn't hurt to take a look around. I knew how things should look, and the sheriff didn't. Maybe I could spot something he hadn't noticed.

As I got closer to the gate I realized it wasn't latched. The sheriff's department must not care very much if anybody went in the yard, since they didn't bother to close the gate.

The dogs stopped at the gate, sniffing all around the area trampled by so many official boots just a couple days earlier. They took a long time to sample everything before they were ready to go in the yard.

I took a deep breath, trying to calm the racing of my heart. I was just going in my mother's backyard. Nothing more. I was going to make sure everything was okay. I had every right to be there, and no one had said I couldn't go in.

So what was I waiting for?

I took another deep breath and blew it out, fluttering my too-long bangs against my forehead. I'd have to take care of that over the weekend.

"Come on guys," I whispered. All the neighbors were inside with the doors and windows closed against the chill of the evening, yet I felt a need to speak as quietly as possible. "Let's check on Grandma's yard."

Sandra Neverall would have had a fit over my calling her Grandma to the dogs. She was still holding out for grandchildren—plural—and was not going to settle for grand-dogs anytime soon. But as I slipped past thirty and started the glide toward forty, it was becoming clear she wasn't going to have a choice. The possibility was still there, but the odds grew longer with each passing year.

The backyard was completely dark. The moon was a narrow crescent high in the sky, and the glow from the streetlight on the corner didn't penetrate the fenced enclosure. The back of Mrs. Sweeney's house was as dark as her kitchen window.

I had a small high-intensity flashlight in my jacket

pocket. I made it a habit to carry it with me whenever I took the dogs out.

I wrapped my fingers around the metal case. It was warm from resting next to my body, and I gripped it tightly. But I didn't take it out and turn it on. No matter how much I told myself I had every right to be there, I didn't want to draw any attention to my presence.

I might believe I was right, but I didn't relish the thought of arguing that point with the sheriff. We'd had that debate before, the discovery of Gregory's body being the latest in a growing list of incidents.

What he didn't know wouldn't hurt me.

I stood still just inside the gate for what felt like an eternity as I waited for my eyes to adjust. I could feel my pupils straining to trap every bit of light as the yard slowly turned from a single dark pit to a dim landscape of grays and blacks, like an old movie with the brightness turned way down.

At last I could see enough to avoid running into the fence or the house in the dark. But I couldn't see much more.

The dogs strained against the leashes, anxious to check out every inch of the yard. I let myself be dragged along behind them toward the back fence.

An unpaved alley ran along the other side of the fence. Once there had been a gate from the yard to the alley, but when my father replaced the fence he'd eliminated the gate as a security measure. I'd noticed several missing boards and put them on my to-do list, but for now the fence wasn't providing much security and I wondered if the dogs were after some animal in the alley.

We were a few feet from the fence when a car turned into the alley, its headlights blinding me. Instinctively, I flattened myself against the fence and ducked down. I tugged on the leashes, forcing the dogs into the shadows with me, and hugged them tight against my pounding chest.

A couple houses over I heard a dog bark, just as I had

the day Gregory was killed. I whispered a warning to Daisy and Buddha to stay quiet, and for once they obeyed a command.

I slipped a shaky hand in my pocket and rewarded them each with a treat. They deserved it.

My eyes recovered a little as the car crept along the alley. Its lights swept along the fence and I was grateful for the solid boards that protected me from exposure. A tire splashed through a pothole, and the lights wavered for a second before resuming their slow progression.

As the car passed my hiding place I watched it through the sliver of space between the boards.

I held my breath and watched the logo of the Pine Ridge Sheriff Department move slowly past.

I swallowed a scream, and forced myself to remain motionless in the dark shadow of the fence.

Had someone seen me despite my precautions? Had they called the sheriff? Was there another car moving into position in front of the house?

And what would happen if they found me here?

chapter 12

I didn't wait around to find out.

As soon as the car reached the end of the alley and turned the corner I wiggled through a hole in the fence, dragging Daisy and Buddha after me.

A dog barked a couple houses over, and another answered. Maybe the deputy was used to the barking; it seemed common in this neighborhood.

I hustled the dogs forward. If the patrol car came back down the alley there was nowhere to hide.

I stumbled in the dark and went down on one knee.

Fear drove me back to my feet in record time. I reached out my right hand and found a chain-link fence lining the alley. Using the fence as a guide I trotted a few yards.

From somewhere behind me I heard a door open. My heart leaped and I nearly stumbled again, but I caught myself with a hand in the mesh of the chain link.

The soft thump of a heavy load echoed down the alley, followed by the clatter of plastic on plastic.

Somebody closing a trash can.

Just some random neighbor dumping their garbage.

I breathed a sigh of relief and hurried on. The patrol car could return at any second; I wasn't safe yet.

The two blocks back to my car were two of the longest blocks I had ever walked. I had to balance the risk of being seen on the road with the risk of walking too near houses where I might be spotted.

When we finally were in sight of the Beetle my heart-beat began to slow.

I loaded the dogs in the car and slid behind the wheel. My hands were shaking with the adrenaline letdown, and I had to brace my arm against the steering wheel to get the key in the ignition.

Mom was waiting up when I got home.

It didn't matter that it was my house. It didn't matter that I was thirty-something, or that I had lived alone in San Francisco and Portland. It didn't matter that I had owned my own company and held my own in the shark tank that was high tech.

In that moment I was fifteen again, trying to sneak in after curfew. And getting caught.

She sat in the overstuffed chair, carefully avoiding my "bed." Dressed in an elegant pair of silk pajamas and a matching robe, she had her legs tucked under her and a book in her hand. A pair of red-framed reading glasses perched on the end of her nose, and she looked at me over their rims, one eyebrow arched in disapproval.

"I thought you went to walk the dogs," she said accusingly.

"I did."

I unclipped the leashes and hung them by the door. The dogs followed me into the kitchen, anxious for their green treats. I didn't disappoint them.

I heard my mother get out of her chair. Her bare feet made almost no sound as she walked to the kitchen and stood in the doorway, her arms crossed over her chest.

"Walking the dogs should involve walking, Georgiana, not driving."

"Sometimes we go to different neighborhoods. Just to get a little variety," I lied.

I put the treats in the cupboard. The dogs tried sad doggy eyes for a minute, then wandered off to their beds, acknowledging defeat on the extra-treats front.

"Variety, Georgiana? They're dogs! They eat the same food every day for years. Why would they need variety?"

She was right, though I wasn't about to admit it. My excuse had sounded pretty lame, even to me.

"I need the variety, Mom. I see the same stretch of road every day. Sometimes several times a day, in fact."

Mom gave a very unladylike snort that clearly expressed her disbelief, but she didn't speak. Instead she simply stood in the kitchen doorway and waited. Just like she did when I was fifteen.

It was a Mom power I should have been able to resist. But somehow, even in her pajamas and bare feet, she had the ability to intimidate me. In my own house.

Then I remembered the one thing that diminished her power: She had a housekeeper! Super-Mom wasn't quite so super after all. Maybe I could get away with a more convincing lie.

"Well," I said, putting on my best you-caught-me face, "I was thinking about going to Tiny's for a beer after we had our walk. But by the time we finished I was tired and I just wanted to come home."

She shook her head. "I guess I should be thankful for small favors," she said. "At least you didn't go hang out at a tavern alone."

I clamped my lower lip between my teeth to keep from smiling. Give her something concrete to disapprove of and she immediately forgot about her other questions. I should have been annoyed at the attitude that a grown woman couldn't go to a local hangout like Tiny's without an escort, but I was too busy being relieved she'd taken my explanation at face value.

"You said you were going to bed," I reminded her.

"I was. But I came in for a cup of tea after my shower and I found your note. You know how it is, Georgiana. I can't sleep when you're out." She shrugged. "So I waited up."

I nodded. She'd always waited up. I didn't know why I thought this time would be any different. "I understand,

Mom. But I'm a grown-up now. You need to relax." I grinned at her, trying to relieve the somber moment. "I'm not your responsibility anymore."

"You'll always be my responsibility, Georgiana," she said tartly. "You're my daughter. And you always will be."

Mom was back on her high horse as she turned and sailed out of the kitchen. A hint of fragrance stirred in her wake, and I finally recognized the scent that had pervaded my house in the last two days.

Joy.

It was Mom's favorite perfume, and it left its mark everywhere. Just like my mother.

I stalled another couple minutes in the kitchen. I listened to Mom moving around in the living room. Then I heard footsteps in the hall and the snap of the bedroom door closing. She'd gone to bed.

I let out the breath I'd been holding.

I had to get Sheriff Mitchell to let her back in her own house.

This was never going to work.

chapter 13

On a normal Saturday morning I would have been in class in Portland. With my licensing exam coming up I *should* have been in class. But there was nothing normal about this Saturday morning.

Mom was up at the crack of dawn and in the bathroom. Again. In spite of her bath the night before she still needed what felt like several hours to get ready to face the day.

I dealt with it by rolling over—as much as I could on the narrow sofa—and pretending I was asleep. It wasn't a great solution.

When she finally emerged and released the sweet-smelling cloud, I stayed put. I pulled a pillow over my head and managed to ignore Mom, Daisy, and Buddha for another half hour.

I considered it a moral victory.

On a normal Saturday my mother would be meeting clients for breakfast, getting ready to show prospective buyers a string of houses. The office at Whitlock Estates would be buzzing by mid-morning with Mom and Gregory zipping in and out.

Nothing was normal for Mom, either.

When I shambled into the kitchen after my shower, she was sitting at the table. Her Bluetooth headset was looped over one ear, and her smartphone was on the table next to her open laptop. She flipped between files on the computer as she talked, occasionally reaching for a steaming mug of coffee.

I stared into the refrigerator. There was too much food in there, and I had to shove things aside to find a carton of yogurt for breakfast.

I carried the yogurt and a cup of coffee back into the living room, away from Mom's rapid-fire instructions to her office staff. All the employees of Whitlock Estates were working from home, and Mom had turned my kitchen table into her command center.

With Gregory gone, I heard her say, it was vital the company appear to be going forward. It was only a matter of time before the metropolitan papers picked up on his death. The remaining agents had to look active and confident if they wanted to keep Whitlock Estates running.

What she didn't say was that they had to keep the company running to preserve her investment. I had seen the prenuptial agreement, and I knew how much of her net worth was tied up in Whitlock Estates.

The thought left me with a knot in my stomach. We'd been through this before. When Dad died, she'd shouldered his debts and somehow managed to hang on to the house. I had been pouring everything I had into Samurai Security and hadn't been able to help.

If Whitlock Estates went down because of Gregory's death it would be the same thing all over again.

For one insane moment I had a vision of the two of us trying to live together to save money. I quickly decided the cost of therapy to recover from the trauma would outweigh any savings.

Whitlock Estates had to survive. The alternative was unthinkable.

The stream of instructions from the kitchen stopped. A few minutes later Mom marched through the living room and into the bedroom. When she emerged she was dressed in an impeccable trouser suit and a pair of stilettos.

I wondered just how many pairs of shoes the woman owned.

She slung her purse over her shoulder and dug out her car keys. "Houses to show," she said. "I don't know when I'll be back."

I heard the deep rumble of the Escalade's engine as she started the car and drove away. I had the house to myself. At least for a little while.

I wandered back into the kitchen. Her laptop was closed, but it still rested on the kitchen table where she had been working.

I can resist anything but temptation, and this was a huge temptation.

Mom's passwords weren't very sophisticated. I was logged on with her user name within three minutes and cruising her files. I don't know what I was looking for exactly. Just something to explain how Gregory and several cases of wine ended up under Mom's house.

But an hour of exploring Mom's files didn't reveal anything more interesting than an unfortunate addiction to bad YouTube videos of too-cute animals and—not surprising— a lot of bookmarked online shoe stores.

My mother's shoe addiction was worse than I thought.

My conscience nagged at me as I poured another cup of coffee and sat back down at the computer. I had no right to paw through Mom's files. They were none of my business and I was invading her privacy and violating her trust.

So, of course I dug deeper. Since the initial barrier was so flimsy, maybe she had a hidden directory with files she wanted secure. None of my usual tricks turned up anything, and I was beginning to believe there wasn't anything to find.

Mom needed a serious security checkup.

I wasn't ready to give up yet. I searched the system files, logged off and back on, and ran several diagnostics.

All the while I listened for the sound of a car in the driveway.

There was something out of balance in the hard drive usage statistics. The capacity of the drive didn't mesh with the space used and available. There were files taking up space somewhere, but I couldn't find them.

I went back to the log-in. I was determined to solve the puzzle of Mom's phantom files. It wasn't about Gregory or his wine any longer. It was all about the challenge.

I was focused so completely on the computer I missed the sound of the car pulling into the driveway.

The knock on the front door startled me. I jumped, jostled the table, and knocked over my coffee cup. A dribble of cold coffee splashed across the keyboard.

I bit back a curse and grabbed a paper towel. I swiped at the keyboard and slammed it closed.

I was halfway to the door when it struck me that it couldn't be Mom. She had her own key.

I opened the door and found Wade Montgomery grinning at me over a cardboard box of donuts.

"Your car was in the driveway," he said as he came in. "So I stopped."

Wade leaned over and kissed me. He tasted of sugar glaze. "Got coffee?" he called back over his shoulder.

It took a few seconds for his question to register.

"Sure." I closed the door and followed him to the kitchen, where he was already pouring himself a cup.

"Uh, help yourself," I said.

"I think I will," he teased, turning to kiss me again.

I laughed and pulled away. "I meant the coffee."

We set the box of donuts on the table and I sat back down next to the laptop. Unable to leave it alone, I flipped it open and went back to cleaning the keyboard.

Wade sat across from me and waited while I finished with the computer.

"Spilled some coffee," I explained. "Just wanted to make sure I got it all cleaned up before it did any damage."

I finished cleaning and checked the keyboard functions. No permanent damage. Reluctantly I logged out and closed the computer. I would have to finish checking the hard drive later.

We made small talk for a few minutes as we ate donuts and drank coffee.

"Aren't you supposed to be in class this morning?" Wade asked.

I nodded. "Yeah, I should be. It's a review session before the licensing exam. But with everything that's going on, I really didn't want to be gone all morning. No telling what Mom would get up to if I wasn't here."

"Speaking of the inimitable Sandra, where is she?" Wade looked around as though he expected her to emerge from the woodwork any minute now. "Her car wasn't out front."

"She said she had some houses to show and didn't know when she'd be back."

Wade studied me for a minute. "How's that going for you?"

He should have known better than to ask. "She's been here two days, Wade, and she's making me crazy. I let her have the bedroom since there's only one, but I didn't count on her taking over the bathroom, too. And she tried to rearrange the living room yesterday! I don't know how long I can handle this."

I shook my head. "I have got to get her back in her own house, or into the new one Gregory built, before I lose my mind."

I glared at Wade, who was struggling to control a grin. "Just what is so funny?"

He tried to look innocent, to hide the smirk on his face, but it didn't work. "Hey, Georgie, you're the one who offered to let her stay here." There was a barely concealed snicker in his voice.

"And what was I supposed to do? Make her move to a hotel in Portland? There isn't anywhere around Pine Ridge that would be acceptable. And the sheriff made it clear she wasn't supposed to leave town. So I really didn't have a choice." I shook my head again. "And I definitely didn't have any other options that wouldn't include the patented Neverall guilt trip."

This time Wade did laugh in spite of my glare. "Now I wouldn't know anything about that, would I, Georgie?"

My glare stayed put. "You were wrong. I said it then, and I'll say it now."

Wade's laughter subsided. "I was seventeen! Of course I was wrong. But what was I supposed to do? And really, Georgie, complicity is a pretty big word for a teenaged girl to go slinging around!"

It was a familiar argument. We covered the same ground every few months, to the point it had become a running joke. Yes, he'd covered for his buddy who was cheating on Sue. And no, I still thought he was wrong.

"Well, you're the one who was best buds with a total horndog."

"Guilty as charged. Josh *was* a total horndog. But he was still my best friend." He held up a hand in mock surrender. "I know. I know. And Sue was your best friend. I am never going to live this down, am I?"

"Never." I smiled.

He sighed dramatically and closed the donut box. "I don't know why I try." He put his coffee cup on the counter. "But how about I give it another go tonight over beer and chicken fingers? About six thirty work for you?"

"Tiny's?" I asked. It was a rhetorical question. In a town the size of Pine Ridge there wasn't any place else.

Wade nodded and picked up the donut box. "I do have some work to do this morning," he said.

I walked him to the door and gave him a quick kiss before promising to meet him at Tiny's for dinner. He waved as he climbed into his sensible hybrid sedan, and I closed the door with a smile on my face.

I was getting used to Wade making me smile. It felt like he had moved from maybe-boyfriend to someone special. He hadn't solved the problem of Sandra, or of Gregory's murder, but he had managed to make me feel better.

I knew it wouldn't last.

chapter 14

The only way to get Sandra Neverall out of my house was to figure out who murdered Gregory Whitlock.

Aside from the sheriff and my mother, that made me the person with the most at stake in this investigation. I couldn't sit around waiting for something to happen; I had to go out and make it happen.

The dogs weren't happy about being left at home, but our adventure the night before had convinced me Daisy and Buddha weren't good choices for investigative pals. I made extravagant promises before I left and hoped they wouldn't hold me to them.

There was one place I hadn't been yet.

Gregory's new house.

I drove out to the new development where Gregory had recently moved. Privately I thought the houses deserved the description of McMansions. They were too big for the sites, built to the limits of the lot lines and crowding against their neighbors. The backyards were tiny, hedged in by tall fences in an attempt to regain a few shreds of privacy from the too-close neighbors.

Gregory's house was one of the largest. A three-car garage stopped short of the side fence, leaving room for a boat or RV to park next to it. Gregory had opted for the boat, a luxury craft whose hull had never even touched the water before its owner was killed.

The front yard was a tiny patch of lawn so green it looked artificial. Since the yard had been bare dirt only a couple weeks earlier it was probably an instant lawn.

I parked at the curb and peered at the house. The front entry was only a few yards from the street. Yellow tape crisscrossed the entry and a notice was posted on the front door. The print was too small to be read from the street, except for the large red letters that said "Warning! Do Not Enter."

Across the street a couple tried to hide their curiosity as they planted flowers in their own patch of bare dirt. A few doors down a teenager with a hose and bucket washed a late-model Beemer, and a block over I could hear the ring of hammers as a construction crew took advantage of the Saturday sunshine.

I was attracting attention just sitting in the car. Attention I didn't need. I wondered if the 'Vette might look more at home in this neighborhood, but dismissed the idea. The 'Vette stood out no matter where I went.

There was nothing to do but start the engine and pull away. If I wanted to check out Gregory's house, this wasn't the way to do it.

The only other clue I had was the wine, and I didn't know a thing about wine. There were lots of wineries in Oregon and they were supposed to be good. So why would Gregory be getting cases shipped to him from Paris?

I could do an Internet search and I probably should. But that wouldn't tell me about the local wine scene. For that I needed to talk to someone who lived in Pine Ridge. Someone who knew everyone in town.

Paula.

The library was a small clapboard building on the corner of the high school campus. Paula had started doing the preschool story hour as a volunteer when her kids were little. Eventually her volunteer career led to a job, which led to her present position as library director.

Pine Ridge was a small town with a tiny library. But thanks to an active interlibrary system, it had access to every collection in the state, and the residents of Pine Ridge took advantage of that connection.

When somebody in Pine Ridge wanted to know about a subject, Paula was the person they turned to. Even in the current age of online searches and Internet databases, Paula was a popular source of information.

Technically the library was only open for a few hours on Saturday morning. But Paula Ciccone didn't operate on technicalities, and neither did her library. She firmly believed a library should be open all the time, and unless she was out of town it was likely she would be there with the doors open. I think she would have tried to keep it open twenty-four/seven if she could convince the City Council.

Sure enough, Paula's car was in the lot at the side of the building and the door was open to the soft afternoon breeze.

Paula looked up and smiled a greeting when I walked in. She was sitting at the computer behind the tall check-out counter, logging in books. The return basket was on the desk next to her terminal instead of in its usual spot on the counter.

"Be with you in a sec, Georgie," she called. "Just got a couple more."

As if to underscore her words, she lifted the last few books from the basket and pushed it across the desk.

I wandered back into the stacks, scanning titles. After my licensing exam maybe I could read something besides textbooks and plumbing manuals. I'd have to ask Paula for some recommendations.

I heard Paula's chair scrape back from the desk, and the rustle of the basket being returned to its spot on the counter. A minute later Paula came up behind me.

"Good to see you, Georgie," she said, hugging me. Paula hugged people the way most people shook hands. She said everyone needed a hug now and then and some people even deserved them. Deserved or not, everyone got a hug from Paula Ciccone.

"What can I do for you?"

I winced. "That obvious, huh?"

She laughed. "Judging from the scowl on your face, something important's brewing. What can I do to help?"

I reached up and smoothed my hands over my face, as though I could wipe away the worries. "You can tell me what you know about wine."

"Wine?" She moved a few steps back and ran her hand along a shelf, tracing the line of numbers on the book spines.

"Here." She pulled a thick volume off the shelf. "This ought to answer your questions."

I took the book from her and held it against my chest. "This should help," I said. "But I need to know who in town really knows his wine."

"Not me," she said. "Barry and I are mostly beer drinkers."

Paula moved toward the little kitchen at the back of the library. "Coffee?" she called over her shoulder. "I need to think about this."

I accepted the cup she poured me and followed her back up to her desk. "Hang on a sec while I check," she said, tapping the keyboard. I leafed through the book she'd given me while I waited, trying to contain my impatience.

I was rewarded with a muttered "There you are," and a satisfied grin from Paula. She looked up from her computer and grinned. "I don't know much about wine, but I know someone who does.

"He's actually kind of a wine snob, to tell the truth. He started checking out books on wine a few years ago, and he's had me get several on interlibrary loan." She rolled her eyes. "He can hardly talk about anything else, and he always has to give me a detailed report of his latest find. But everybody needs a hobby, I guess."

"Can I talk to him? Do you know where he is?"

"Let me call him first and be sure he's okay with me giving you his name and number. I know"—she shook her head—"it's not like I'm giving you his medical records or something, but I'd still feel funny if he didn't want anybody to know his private business."

Paula gave me a puzzled look. "Why is this so important all of a sudden? I never knew you to care much about wine. What gives? Is your mother driving you so crazy you need to drink? I'd have thought hard liquor would be more to the point."

I rolled my eyes. "It's about Gregory. Those boxes under the house were cases of wine, and I need to find out why they were there."

"Are you sure you want to get into this?" Paula shook her head. "The sheriff won't like it, Georgie. Just let him do his job. He'll get to the bottom of whatever it is."

"Look, I'm not interfering. But I have every right to know what happened to Gregory, if only for my mom's sake. If I can figure out who did this, she can move back home. I can't take her living with me. I can't. I really can't."

"Of course you can. You lived with her for years while you were growing up. Meanwhile, Fred Mitchell is quite capable of solving this thing. Why can't you let him?"

"Because, Paula. I have a stake in this. I didn't like the guy, but he was almost"—I nearly choked on the word—"my *stepfather*."

She looked skeptical.

"And the sooner this gets resolved, the sooner my mother can go back to her own house." I pleaded with her. "Please, Paula. It's been two days and I am already losing my mind."

Paula's mouth twitched. I knew I'd gotten to her.

She nodded. "Okay. But I still have to call him first."

It didn't sound to me like the guy was very private about his hobby if he was bending Paula's ear in the middle of the library. But that was Paula, considerate of everyone.

I agreed to her terms.

Mom wasn't home when I pulled into the driveway. I hoped it was a good sign that she was busy closing a deal. It would be a much-needed boost for her, and for Whitlock Estates.

The laptop was where I had left it, tempting me to try again. But my mother could be home any minute and I didn't want a repeat of this morning's panic. I would have to wait.

Instead I dragged out my books and notes and tried to study.

Mom still wasn't home when I left for dinner.

chapter 15

When I got to Tiny's, a few couples were already using the postage-stamp-sized dance floor and the Saturday-night crowd was warming up for a long night.

Tiny's was that kind of joint. The clientele was locals and everyone knew everyone else, and on weekends most of the population of Pine Ridge showed up sometime during the night.

The over-twenty-one population anyway.

When I was a kid Tiny's was a forbidden place, full of secrets. Now I knew better; it was nothing more exotic than a local tavern with fried food and draft beer.

Wade saw me come in. He smiled warmly, waving me over to the table he'd staked out in the back, away from the jukebox. Two frosty mugs waited on the table.

I smiled back and made my way through the crowd, pausing occasionally to say hello to people I knew. I was part of this town now, and I liked it.

I had been part of Pine Ridge before, but then I had been Doc Neverall's daughter. Now I was an adult with my own identity and my own relationships.

I still didn't know exactly where Wade fit in that identity. He had been my high school sweetheart for a few months—before the infamous "complicity" episode—and we'd been dating since I returned to Pine Ridge. But we were still taking it slow and trying to find our way.

There was something between us. How much of a thing? I wasn't sure, though I suspected it was becoming a big thing. Still, I wasn't sure Wade deserved my poor track record when it came to romance.

Blake Weston's death still weighed on my mind. I had been willing to believe the worst of him. I had been wrong and Blake died before I could give him the apology he deserved.

Worse, if I hadn't believed the lies Stan Fischer, my old mentor at Samurai, told me, maybe Blake wouldn't have been killed.

For now, though, Wade Montgomery and I were spending some time together and trying to figure out if a lady plumber and an accountant/City Councilman were a good match.

I was beginning to hope they were.

I made it to the table and greeted Wade with a hug. "Thanks," I said. I slid into the seat next to him and shrugged out of my Windbreaker, draping it carelessly over the back of the chair.

It would be a good night for crowd watching, and with our backs to the wall we had a view of the room and the front door.

I picked up the mug and took a long drink. The cold beer slid down my throat. The chill spread through my stomach and I realized I hadn't eaten since the donuts that morning.

"Did you order?" I asked.

"Of course! Chicken and fries, right?"

I nodded. Tiny's had the best chicken fingers I'd ever tasted, and I'd been looking forward to them ever since Wade suggested them.

The jukebox was cranked up but we were far enough away to talk without shouting. I decided no one could hear our conversation.

"Wade, can I ask you something?"

His face clouded up. "Ask all you want. But you know there are questions I won't answer."

I nodded. Wade was famous around town for his discretion. He was the accountant for many of the individuals and businesses in Pine Ridge and he was proud that he had earned their trust. He wouldn't do anything to endanger his reputation.

"Fair enough. You know I witnessed Mom and Gregory's prenup, so I know a lot—way more than I wanted to know, to tell the truth—about their finances. Mom insisted that I needed to read everything before they signed it. She said since I was an only child I should know what was what."

"I agreed with her."

I shot Wade a hard look. "You knew?"

He shrugged. "She asked me to explain a couple things before she showed them to you. Just to clarify some terms. Wanted to be sure she understood exactly what she was showing you.

"I told her I thought it was a good idea for her to be straight with you about her finances. I didn't point out that she should have done that with you years ago when your dad died. I think she knew that and was trying to avoid making the same mistake this time."

Wade colored and covered his face with one hand as though he couldn't believe the blunder he'd made. "That's not what I meant. Not that this was the same situation, though I guess it is now."

I reached over and pulled his hand away. "I know what you meant. Don't worry about it. This is way different."

"Sorry," he muttered.

"Anyway"—I plunged ahead—"there was this thing on the list of investments called Veritas Partnership. It was something of Gregory's, one of the few things he wasn't putting in joint ownership."

Wade nodded.

"That struck me as kind of strange. They were pooling

most of their assets, except Mom was keeping the house and Gregory was keeping this Veritas thing, whatever it was."

Wade cocked his head to one side and glanced around the room. He took a sip of his beer, looked back at me, and shrugged.

"People choose to maintain separate property for a lot of reasons, Georgie. Why did your mom keep the house separate? Did she say?"

"Because I'm buying it. She said something about her not wanting anyone else to be involved in a transaction between the two of us. Said that part was nobody else's business."

"And?"

"And nothing! Gregory didn't have any family. Mom told me he was an only child and his parents died several years ago. His ex-wife remarried some big exec and they live in Japan or Hong Kong or something, and he never had any kids. So that has nothing to do with it."

What my mother had actually said was "We're Gregory's family now," which had completely creeped me out. It was even creepier now that Gregory had been murdered.

"Maybe not. But there could be a lot of other reasons." He shrugged elaborately and held his hands out to his sides. "Maybe it was something your mother didn't want to be part of, or maybe they disagreed on how to handle whatever investment Veritas held. Or maybe it wasn't Gregory's decision at all. Did you ever think of that?"

Wade's expression was deliberately neutral. He didn't say anything more, just sat back and waited while I thought about what he'd said.

"So you're telling me Gregory didn't have control of Veritas, and he couldn't make my mother a part of it."

Wade widened his eyes in a parody of innocence. "Me?" He put a hand against his chest. "Did I say that? I don't think so. I was just speculating about the reasons any random person might choose to keep a piece of property separate in a prenuptial agreement.

"I never said that was the reason a specific person, like Gregory Whitlock, made that choice."

His denial was so phony it was laughable. But it was a denial. If anyone ever asked, I could truthfully say that Wade had told me nothing about Gregory Whitlock's financial affairs. Or about Veritas.

I wanted to laugh, but I went along. "Why, you're quite right, Mr. CPA Montgomery. You didn't mention Mr. Whitlock even once. The only person you mentioned by name was my mother." I nodded in his direction and raised my glass. "To your discretion."

Our food arrived, the chicken radiating near-volcanic heat. The heady aroma of hot grease and salt assaulted my senses. My mouth watered. I fanned a couple fries and popped them in my mouth.

I instantly regretted it.

A quick gulp of beer cooled my mouth.

"Hungry?" Wade asked, arching one eyebrow.

He knew that annoyed me because I couldn't do it. As a teenager I'd stood in front of the mirror for hours trying to make just one brow arch without success. Both brows shot up making me look like a startled owl. It was a lost cause.

I pushed the food a few inches away, as though that would lessen the temptation. I spread a napkin on the table and picked up one fry at a time with my fingertips, dropping them onto the napkin individually so they could cool to a safe eating temperature.

While I waited I went back to my questions. "Okay, you didn't tell me anything. I get that. But I'm guessing that Veritas was more than just Gregory. And I'm guessing my mother wasn't one of the others. But just what is Veritas? If there are other investors, it must still be going."

Wade nodded for me to go on.

"And what kind of a name is that anyway? Veritas!" I held up a hand to forestall a reply. "I don't expect you to answer that one. It was a rhetorical question. I know it's Latin for *truth*, but how pretentious is that? The only thing

I can figure is the old saying *'En vino veritas,'*—'In wine, truth.' It seems like the kind of name Gregory would give a wine company."

The fries had cooled enough to handle and I popped a couple in my mouth. I knew my mother was right and I couldn't continue to eat like this forever without ballooning into something resembling the Goodyear blimp, but Tiny's fries were worth every nutritional hit I took.

Wade took a bite of chicken before he replied. "I suppose someone might make that connection."

"It would be interesting to know who else was involved with Veritas. They might know something important."

Wade shook his head. "I'd be curious to know, too."

"He didn't tell you?"

"I didn't work for Veritas," he said around a mouthful of chicken.

Another question was forming when I saw Sue come through the front door and look around. She spotted us in the back, waved, and headed our direction.

Question time was over.

If your showerhead is running slow, or the water flow is erratic, try cleaning the showerhead with vinegar to remove the mineral buildup that is the likely culprit. Remove the showerhead and soak it in a bowl of vinegar overnight, then rinse it in warm water, check to see the blockage is removed, and reinstall it. If you can't remove the showerhead, try treating it in place. Fill a sturdy plastic bag with vinegar and fasten the filled bag over the showerhead with a rubber band or two, making sure that the vinegar is soaking the bottom of the showerhead. Leave it on overnight, remove it the next morning, and run the shower to clean the vinegar from the showerhead. The flow should be markedly improved.

—A Plumber's Tip from Georgiana Neverall

chapter 16

Sue slid into a seat across the table from me. "Wade said you'd be here so I thought I'd crash the party." She grinned and snagged a fry from my basket. "Oooh, still hot. Is my timing good or what?"

She munched happily and grinned at me. "So what's new in Sandra world?"

I rolled my eyes. "Nothing's new. It's all the same stuff." I sighed. "I just wish I could have my house back."

Sue flagged down a waitress and ordered her own beer. She turned back to me with a knowing grin. "I don't think I'm supposed to know this," she said, "but you just might get your wish."

"Really? You mean it?"

I practically shouted, and Sue quickly shushed me. I glanced around, but the Tiny's crowd was getting noisier with each passing minute. No one had noticed.

"I was just in Fred's office," she continued. "I stopped to see if he wanted to come with me."

Annoyance flashed through me. Fred Mitchell was the reason I was in this predicament to begin with. Having dinner with him wasn't on my list of fun things to do with a Saturday night.

"He said he was busy and he couldn't, but maybe he'd try to catch up with me a little later, so you don't have to be like that. Anyway, he's not *trying* to make you miserable."

"Well, he's doing a heckuva job for a guy who's not even trying," I muttered.

"Oh, stop whining," Sue teased.

"You'd whine, too, if you had Sandra Neverall in your house." I crossed my arms over my chest and lowered my chin. I knew I looked like a pouty child, and it was how I felt. The adult Georgiana knew Fred was just doing his job and even felt sorry for him, but the kid Georgie still resented her mother's forced intrusion.

"That's what I'm trying to tell you! When I was leaving he got a phone call. I was outside the office and I could hear him talking. I don't know who was on the phone, but I heard him ask if it meant he could release the crime scene.

"The crime scene in question is your mom's house, Georgie. If he can release the crime scene, then you get your wish to have your house back."

"That is probably the best news I've had all week."

"Promise me you'll act surprised? I'm sure I'm not supposed to know, and I'm *really* sure I wasn't supposed to tell you."

I nodded, grinning widely.

The waitress appeared with Sue's beer, and I was so happy with the news she'd brought me I paid for the beer and left a hefty tip.

I was going to get my life back!

Be careful what you wish for.

We were celebrating my impending release with another round of beers—on me—when my cell phone rang. The phone was in my jacket pocket and I couldn't actually hear it over the noise of the crowd and the jukebox, but I felt it buzzing against my back.

The number wasn't familiar, though it was local, and the two most likely people to call me were sitting within a few feet. Still, I hadn't heard from my mom since early morning. Maybe she had a phone problem and was calling from a landline.

I flipped open the phone.

"Georgiana? Georgiana, is that you?"

"Yes, Mother." I rolled my eyes. Wade grinned, and Sue chuckled softly. "You called my cell phone, who did you think it would be?"

"I need you. Right now. You have to come down here." There was genuine anger in her voice, an emotion she seldom indulged.

"Where is *here*, Mom? And what do you need?"

"I need you to get me out of here!"

"Where?" Even taking into account what had happened to Gregory, my patience with her demands was growing thin. Whatever she was mad about, it wasn't my fault and I wasn't going to let her take it out on me. "If you really need my help, Mother, you need to tell me what you need and where you are. And you need to ask nicely."

I felt an instant of triumph at being able to turn one of her lectures back on her.

There was a moment of silence. Sandra Neverall didn't apologize easily, but I could be patient.

When she finally spoke the anger had turned into an icy fury more intense than I had ever heard. And I knew it wasn't directed at me.

"I'm at the sheriff's office, Georgiana. These sons-of-bitches just arrested me. They think I killed Gregory."

chapter 17

I heard a man in the background tell Mom her time was up, and the connection ended abruptly. I was left listening to dead air.

"Georgie?" Wade put his arm around me. "What's wrong? Are you okay? Is your mother all right?"

I shook my head and buried my face in Wade's shoulder. It couldn't be true.

I pulled away and glared at Sue. "Is this your idea of a joke? Telling me my mom could go home, and then this! It's not funny!"

Sue stared, her eyes wide. "What?"

"Do you think this is a funny joke for you and your boyfriend to cook up? Come in here with your big secret and let me think everything was going to get better? Huh?"

"What are you talking about? That was your mom, right? What has Fred got to do with it?" Sue was bewildered by my abrupt mood change, and she looked like she was about to cry. "What happened?"

Wade gripped my shoulder and pulled me around to face him. "Georgie." His voice was low and hard. "What in the hell do you think you're doing?"

I glanced at Sue and back at Wade, instantly ashamed of the wild accusations I'd thrown around. Sue was my best friend.

I shook my head and buried my face in Wade's shoulder again. I was afraid I was going to cry. I hated to cry, especially in front of people.

"Let's get out of here," I said to Wade's shoulder. "I'll explain when we get outside."

I felt Wade move his head and look in Sue's direction. I didn't dare look or I would lose it.

"Okay," Wade said softly.

Without looking at either of them I grabbed my jacket off the back of the chair and pushed through the crowd to the door. I didn't look back until I was in the parking lot leaning against the roof of the Beetle.

Sue stopped a few feet away and Wade stood between us like the referee at a prize fight.

"You better tell us what that was all about, Georgie," Wade said.

I laid my arms across the Beetle's roof and rested my forehead against them. The metal was cold against my arms. It felt good.

I worked to control my breathing. Slow deep breaths, in and out, practicing the martial arts techniques that allowed me to control my temper.

Most of the time.

"I'm sorry," I said. "You have to know I didn't mean any of those things." I took another deep breath. "Me and my damned temper."

"Swearing, Georgie? Is it that bad?" To my immense relief, I heard a faint whisper of amusement in Sue's voice. Because of Barry, I didn't swear on the job, so I stopped swearing off the job, too.

"Yeah, Sue. It is. It really is."

I pushed myself away from the car and turned to face my two best friends. They had stood by me when I'd been a suspect in Blake's murder; they would stick by me now.

"Fred is involved, Sue. I'm sorry for what I said, but he is involved." I drew another deep breath and slowly let it out. "He just arrested my mom for Gregory's murder."

The stricken look on Sue's face was enough proof for me. She hadn't known anything about Sheriff Mitchell's plan to arrest my mother.

Wade wrapped me in his arms and held me tight, offering the comfort of his embrace. I felt Sue move closer and her arms wrapped around me.

How could I have doubted her even for a second?

"I am such a jerk," I said.

"Don't sweat it," Sue answered.

"So what are we going to do?" That was Wade, always practical.

I wished I had a good answer.

"I guess the first thing I need to do is go to the sheriff's office and find out what's going on."

I dug in my pocket for my car keys, but Wade reached for them and stuffed them in his jacket. "I'll take you. We can come back for your car later, or Sue and I can come get it. You're not driving right now."

I didn't argue.

I walked into the sheriff's office with Wade and Sue on either side of me. It felt like there should have been Western-movie-showdown music in the background as we pushed through the front doors and moved across the lobby.

The deputy at the desk spotted us and picked up the phone. Before I could give him my name, Fred Mitchell emerged from the back.

"Come in, please," he said, opening the door into the offices.

He didn't say anything about my companions and they stuck with me. If he didn't want them along he was going to have to throw them out. He showed us to a private office instead of the bare interview room where I'd been the day before, and waved us into a row of side chairs facing the desk.

Sheriff Mitchell took his place behind the desk. He looked even more tired and worn—if that was possible—than the last time I'd seen him. He didn't meet my gaze.

Silence grew until it filled the room. No one wanted to speak first.

I bit back my anger and tried to calm my breathing. I couldn't afford to unleash my temper on the man who was holding my mother in a jail cell.

"I'm sure I know why you're all here," the sheriff said. "My deputy apparently allowed your mother unauthorized access to a telephone. That's unfortunate, but"—he shrugged, his shoulders barely moving as though he was too tired to expend the energy—"things happen."

"The prosecutor's office has filed charges against Sandra Neverall in the death of Gregory Whitlock," he went on. "She'll be arraigned on Monday morning. In the meantime, she will be held here in Pine Ridge, so long as there are no other prisoners."

I remembered when the sheriff had arrested the Gladstones; Rachel had been jailed in Portland because Pine Ridge didn't have facilities for both male and female prisoners.

There was something in the sheriff's speech that sounded rehearsed. I was sure he'd said similar things many times, though I doubted he mentioned murder very often. I replayed his statement in my head, examining his words.

It was what he hadn't said that caught my attention. He said the prosecutor had filed charges, not that his office had arrested Mom.

"She'll need a lawyer, Miss Neverall. I would suggest you might be in a better position than she is to look for a good one."

"Can I see her?" I asked. It was the first thing I trusted myself to say.

"I'll arrange it," he answered. "Most places have rules and regulations about visitors and such. But since she's the only prisoner I don't see why not."

He stood up and walked around the desk. "If you want to wait here, I'll see what I can do."

The minute he was out of the office I turned to Wade.

"Do you know a good lawyer? The only ones I've heard of around here were the Gladstones. And since they're in prison for killing Martha Tepper and trying to kill me . . ."

"No trial lawyers," he answered. "Most of the guys I work with specialize in trusts and estates, that sort of thing. But I'm sure I can get you some names."

"What can I do, Georgie?" Sue asked.

I turned to look at her. "I honestly don't know. I don't know what I need to do besides find her a lawyer as fast as possible." I wanted to ask her about what Fred Mitchell has said, but I didn't want to talk about it in his office.

I knew how much he liked his little recorder.

The sheriff returned quickly and motioned for me to follow him. He led me to an area where I had never been before: the jail cells.

The Pine Ridge sheriff's station was a modern facility. The cells were more like rooms, except the doors had heavy locks and the glass in the windows was reinforced with steel wires.

The furnishings left a lot to be desired, however. A sturdy metal bunk was bolted to the wall, its legs embedded in the concrete floor. There was a stainless-steel plumbing unit on another wall with a sink and toilet. Everything appeared unbreakable.

Mom sat on the bunk, her hands in her lap. She had on the clothes she'd worn to work that morning, all except her shoes. I guess letting a prisoner keep her stilettos was a bad idea, but somehow Mom's feet in a pair of too-big white crew socks brought tears to my eyes.

Or maybe it was the sting of the harsh disinfectant that pervaded the building.

I stood in the doorway. I didn't know where to look or where to put my hands. I settled for sticking them in my pockets.

"How are you doing, Mom?" Stupid question! She was in jail charged with the murder of her fiancé. How did I think she was doing?

"Get me out of here, Georgiana. I can't possibly stay in this place. It's ridiculous."

Mom was back to issuing commands and expecting them to be followed.

As much as I hated to admit it, she made me proud.

chapter 18

"I'll do what I can, Mom. But the first thing we need is a lawyer. Is there anyone you would like me to call?"

She never got a chance to answer.

Sheriff Mitchell came down the corridor and took me by the arm. He walked me quickly back toward the front of the building, and I heard the cell door close behind us.

"Your mother's arraignment will be Monday morning," he said. His voice echoed loudly in the empty corridor, with no sign of the fatigue I'd seen earlier. "We don't have any women's jumpsuits in our stores, so you may bring her some clean clothes if you wish. No belts, no laced shoes. My advice would be to bring jeans, T-shirts, warm socks—"

He stopped suddenly as the door at the end of the corridor opened. In the doorway stood a young man in an off-the-rack charcoal gray suit, a crisp white shirt, and a paisley silk tie. I guessed his age at about thirty, though his pale hair—only slightly longer than the sheriff's military buzz—made him look younger.

"Vernon." The sheriff nodded curtly. He wasn't surprised to see him, whoever he was.

The younger man continued toward us, oblivious to the chill in the sheriff's attitude. "Evening, Sheriff. Is she here?"

The sheriff nodded.

"Douglas Vernon, Deputy Prosecutor." He extended his hand to me. "And you are?"

"Just leaving," the sheriff said, his voice tight. He shoved me ahead of him and marched me through the open door.

Before I could speak, he turned and went back through the heavy security door, slamming it firmly behind him.

The deputy at the front desk pointed me toward the interview room where I'd been before. I shrugged and went that direction.

Sue was waiting.

"Time to go." She took my arm and pulled me toward the front door.

I looked around for Wade. "He's in the car," Sue whispered, dragging me as fast as we could without running.

We ran to Wade's car and Sue dove in the backseat. Wade pulled out into the empty street while I was still fastening my seat belt.

"Am I a fugitive or something?"

Wade's laugh wasn't amused. "Now we know why your mom was arrested on a Saturday evening. Douglas Vernon." He looked over at me, then back at the road. "Did he see you?"

"Yeah. The sheriff grabbed me out of Mom's"—I swallowed hard—"cell and marched me down the hall about the time Vernon came in. He introduced himself, but the sheriff hustled me out of there before I could tell him who I was. Which was kind of weird and uncomfortable. I got the impression the sheriff doesn't like the guy very much."

"What was the first thing I ever told you about Fred Mitchell, Georgie? Do you remember?"

I forced my thoughts away from the image of my mother in a jail cell and tried to remember my conversation with Wade the first time I had encountered Fred Mitchell.

"That he doesn't like people interfering with his work? Something like that." It was coming back to me now. I'd wanted Wade to talk to the sheriff about Martha Tepper's disappearance. "But I was right about that, Wade."

Wade nodded. "He didn't exactly welcome your involvement, did he? Now imagine how happy he'd be about that if you were someone he couldn't brush off or ignore."

A light bulb went off in my head. "Like the Deputy Prosecutor?"

"Yeah. Like the Deputy Prosecutor."

I got the picture and it wasn't a pretty one.

Besides being a suspect in a murder, my mother was caught in the middle of a testosterone battle.

"We need to figure out what to do next," I said. "You guys want to come back to my place?"

When I unlocked my front door I was met by the unmistakable scent of Joy. In just two days Mom had managed to imprint her signature fragrance on my house and my life. For one insane moment I expected her to come sailing out of the bathroom on a cloud of Joy-scented steam.

Instead I was mugged by a pair of Airedales looking for a doggy bag of dinner scraps. How they knew I had gone out for dinner was unclear, but they obviously did.

Daisy and Buddha were disappointed on the leftovers front, but Sue's arrival with a pocketful of treats more than made up for it. Sue was a sucker for every dog she met, and doubly so for the ones she knew well.

Daisy fluttered and flirted like her fictional namesake, while Buddha waited patiently for his share of the treats. I am convinced animals live up—or down—to their names. It's one reason I'll never have a dog named Muffy.

We settled around the kitchen table after I let the dogs out into the backyard. The evening was cool but not cold and I left the door open for them. In Airedale world that was a huge privilege.

Mom's laptop was where I had left it that afternoon, but I couldn't work at unlocking its secrets while Wade and Sue were there. It could wait until after they left.

I filled the two of them in on the little bit of information I had gained from my visit to Paula, which wasn't much more than the promise of a name, if her guy agreed to talk to me.

My mother had left her mark on my kitchen again. In the middle of my normally bare table she'd put a metal holder with paper napkins and salt and pepper shakers.

Wade took a napkin out of the holder and folded it into smaller and smaller squares as he listened. He unfolded it and flattened it on the table, then began to accordion-pleat the soft paper.

His fidgeting continued as we talked, until he suddenly wadded it into a tight ball and pitched it at the wastebasket. It bounced off the rim but he ignored it. He slapped his palm against the table and cursed softly.

"Wade?" Sue looked at him, her brow furrowed.

"I wish I could help, Georgie. I really do. But Gregory never told me who else was part of Veritas. You were right, by the way, it is about the wine. Gregory and several other individuals formed an investment group to buy wine. Gregory put a cellar in his new house and they were going to store it until the prices went up, then sell it at a profit.

"Gregory was quite pleased with himself about the wine cellar. He planned to bill the partnership for the storage so he'd get a bigger slice of the profits. Not that that's going to happen now."

"But if it was supposed to be stored in his cellar, what were those cases doing under Sandra's house?" Sue asked.

It was the same question we'd all been asking each other and ourselves since I found Gregory's body.

And we were no closer to an answer than we had been then.

I found some cookies in the cupboard and made tea.

The conversation continued, but we soon realized we were talking in the same circles over and over. No one had anything new to add. We went over the same ground, trying to figure out what kind of evidence could implicate Sandra. None of us had an answer, and we were all sagging in our chairs. Even the dogs had given up their outdoor explorations and wandered off to their beds.

Sue yawned and stretched. "I give up," she said. "I need to go home and get some sleep. Unless," she added hastily, "you need me to stay."

I considered her offer and shook my head. "You've already done a lot, and I appreciate it, even if I don't act like it sometimes." I gave her an embarrassed grin. "You'll be happier in your own bed. But thanks."

"Do you want me to take the dogs? You could be pretty busy tomorrow."

I turned her down, and she dragged herself out the door, promising to call me in the morning, and extracting my promise to call her anytime day or night, if something important happened.

Wade left a few minutes after Sue. He hesitated, as though he, too, was going to offer to stay, then thought better of it. Instead, he asked if I wanted him to take some clothes to my mother.

I'd forgotten about the clothes in our hasty retreat from the sheriff's station. Mom would need something to sleep in, and something to wear in the morning.

Wade stood discreetly in the hallway while I packed a bag with Mom's casual wear. I found underwear, a couple pairs of designer jeans, and some canvas espadrilles, but nothing even close to a T-shirt.

"I don't think my mother knows what a plain old T-shirt is," I hollered to Wade as I pawed my way through the cashmere sweater sets and silk blouses that hung in what used to be my closet. "There isn't anything in here that doesn't need to be hand washed or dry-cleaned."

"Is there something I can do to help?" he called back.

"Nope." I dragged the little gym bag into the hallway and opened the storage closet. "I'm bigger than she is," I said. "But she'll just have to cope." I pulled a three-pack of plain white T-shirts out of my stash and added them to the bag. That would hold her for a couple days. By then she should be home.

I hoped.

I found a clean sweatshirt stacked in my workout room and put it on top of the T-shirts before zipping the bag closed and handing it to Wade.

"Are you sure about this?" I asked. "I could take it myself."

He shook his head. "It's practically on my way home," he fibbed gallantly.

It was actually a couple miles out of his way, but I didn't argue. If he delivered the bag I could start on the laptop that much sooner. And it meant I didn't have to risk running into Douglas Vernon.

When I closed and locked the door behind Wade, I was finally alone in the house for the first time in three days. And it felt lonely.

That was the real reason I had turned down Sue's offer to take the dogs: I needed some company. With Mom missing, the house echoed in ways it never had before. As irritating as she was, I had quickly grown used her presence.

Not that I wanted her here all the time. It would only take a day, probably less, for us to drive each other nuts again. But I wanted her in her own house, not one owned by the county.

I wanted her out of jail.

And it looked like I was going to have to be the one to get her sprung.

I made a pot of coffee and put the package of cookies in easy reach on the table before I opened Mom's laptop.

It occurred to me that the sheriff and the prosecutor probably would want to seize the computer as evidence if they knew where it was. I might have only a few hours to crack its secrets.

I poured myself a cup of coffee and sat down.

It was going to be a long night.

chapter 19

Acid burned in my stomach, a combination of too much coffee, too many cookies, and exhaustion. My eyes burned and itched with lack of sleep and my back ached from the immobile hours hunched over the stubborn laptop.

But I had won. There on the screen was a folder labeled "Veritas."

I stood up to get a thumb drive from my desk. My right leg was asleep, the result of my cramped posture, and I nearly toppled over.

I caught myself on the back of my chair. Within seconds the tingling pain of returning circulation spread down my leg. I gritted my teeth and inched forward until I could reach the drive.

I knew better. When I ran Samurai Security I'd insisted on ergonomic chairs and regular stretch breaks for my employees and for myself. It was just good business. So was the masseuse who made office calls.

As I gingerly lowered myself into my non-ergonomic kitchen chair I longed for that masseuse. On-call massage therapists were not the sort of amenity you found in a town the size of Pine Ridge.

Especially not at—I glanced at the clock and groaned—four o'clock in the morning.

I plugged in the thumb drive and quickly copied the

file folder. I verified the copy and made sure the data was good. With the drive stowed back in my desk drawer away from prying eyes, I breathed a sigh of relief.

Even if the sheriff or the prosecutor came looking for Mom's computer, I had the data I needed. But I was too exhausted to try to decipher the files. That could wait until morning. Well, *later* in the morning.

I stood in the shower and let the water run over me for several minutes. The warm water soothed my aching muscles, and the antacids I'd popped were beginning to calm my stomach.

I dragged myself from the shower and dressed in the pajamas I'd borrowed from Sue. I still owed her for those. I'd have to remember to pay her next time I saw her.

Time for bed.

The bedroom door was ajar, and I pushed it open. The bed was made with a precision I never achieved, the comforter hanging straight and even and the pillows piled artfully across the head of the bed.

It wasn't my bed. It was my mother's. And I couldn't sleep in it.

I staggered out to the couch, wrapped myself in the spare blanket that had been folded over the arm, and closed my eyes.

I tried to ignore the ringing phone, but Daisy stuck her wet nose in my face and insisted I wake up and make the annoying noise stop at once.

The phone was only inches from my head. It took a second for me to register why I had slept with the phone next to me.

I was instantly awake, my heart pounding.

I snatched up the cell phone and flipped it open. "Hello?"

"Morning, Georgie." Paula's voice was overly cheery, the kind of voice you use when you visit someone in the hospital. Obviously she had heard about my mother.

Relief was like a rush of ice water through my body,

chasing away the adrenaline-fueled heat. I relaxed back against the couch cushions and took a deep breath.

"Hi, Paula. What's up?" I felt a quaver in my voice, a reaction to the emotional roller-coaster ride.

"You okay, Georgie? You sound a little shaky." Paula's obvious concern touched me. It was good to have friends who actually cared about you.

"Late night," I answered. And a long day ahead, but I pushed the thought from my mind. If I dwelled on it I would pull the blanket over my head and not come out for a week.

"I heard. I don't know what the sheriff is thinking." Her voice rose in indignation now that the subject had been broached. "Your mother wouldn't hurt a fly!"

I agreed. Mother would never stoop to physically harming someone. Verbal torture was much more her style.

"Sorry," Paula said. "I swore I wasn't going to butt in. It just makes me so mad!"

"It's okay, really. I appreciate the moral support. But that wasn't what you called for, was it?"

"No, no, it wasn't." She seemed to give herself a mental shake. "I called about my wine guy. You are still interested in talking to him, aren't you?"

I stood up and moved into the kitchen, rummaging in my desk for a pencil and paper. This might be the break I needed.

"More than ever," I answered.

"Okay. He said I could give you his name and number and you could call him to set up a meeting. He's a bit of a character, Georgie, but don't let that put you off. He's not a bad guy."

My heart sank. If Paula, who was one of the sweetest people on the planet, thought this guy was a character, there was no telling what he might actually be like.

Still, I needed to talk to someone who knew about wine and who might know others in town who were interested in wine. I made myself a promise to withhold judgment.

Maybe he wouldn't be so bad.

"His name's William Robinson. And he hates being called Bill or Will—especially not Will. Says his name is William, or Mr. Robinson." She stifled a giggle, but I heard it anyway. "Yeah, he's kind of stuffy. But he's studied a lot about wine, so maybe he can help you."

I scribbled the number she gave me next to where I'd written William Robinson in capital letters, and thanked her for the introduction.

By the time I hung up I was wide awake, but it was too early to call a complete stranger, especially one who insisted on being called William.

I let the dogs out and made us all breakfast. Yogurt, cereal, and more fresh coffee for me, dog food for them.

I got the usual accusatory looks when they examined the contents of their bowls. "You should be grateful," I told them. "I'm sure there are starving dogs somewhere that would be happy to have that food."

They weren't impressed.

No one had come pounding on my door demanding Mom's laptop, though I expected a visit from Sheriff Mitchell or one of his deputies at any time. I flipped open the machine and brought up the Veritas folder. Now that I knew where it was hidden it took only a few keystrokes.

In the folder I found a file of correspondence and several spreadsheets. There was also a backup of an e-mail file.

I was extracting the e-mail correspondence when the phone rang again.

"I found a lawyer," Wade said without preamble.

"On Sunday morning?" I was impressed by Wade's efficiency and touched by his concern.

"An old college friend. He's an associate at a big firm in Portland, but he just called me back and said one of the senior partners has agreed to advise him. I hope you don't mind, but I went ahead and arranged for him to come out this afternoon and talk to your mom. I figured she would need some time with him before the arraignment."

I felt as though a giant weight had been lifted off my shoulders. Mom had a lawyer. One less thing for me to have to worry about.

"Mind? Are you crazy? This might just make up entirely for the whole complicity thing. Thank you!"

Wade chuckled, the sound sending a flood of warmth through me. Whatever this thing was between us, it was definitely getting stronger. The man was starting to look like a keeper.

The thought scared me. My experience with romance was limited, and the results were mixed at best. And I definitely didn't have time to think about it right now.

"I dropped the bag of clothes off with the sheriff on my way home," Wade said. "Sandra was still with Vernon so I didn't get to see her, but judging from Mitchell's smirk I don't think Vernon was getting much of anything."

It was my turn to smile. My mother could out-stubborn anybody I knew. If she didn't want to answer Vernon's questions she'd refuse to talk to him, and there wouldn't be any real way of budging her. I hoped.

"What time is your friend coming out?"

"He said he'd be here around one. He was going to call the sheriff and make sure he could meet with his client. He said he could talk to us after he sees her.

"Does that work for you?"

"I'll make it work," I answered. "I have a little news myself. Paula called a little bit ago. She knows a wine guy here in town, and he's willing to talk to me. I thought maybe he might know something about Veritas. I know it sounds like a pretty long shot, but we have to start somewhere."

"That's great!" Wade's enthusiasm sounded a bit forced, but I was getting used to fake-cheery from my friends. At least they were trying to be supportive.

"I have to call him, but I've kind of been stalling." I had an idea. "Would you go with me?" I asked. "To talk to him? I don't know him, and it might be easier for both of us if there was another person there. I'll ask him if it's okay," I added quickly. I didn't want to just spring Wade on the guy, but I could use the moral support.

"Sure. Just let me know when and where."

"Thanks, Wade." My throat constricted unexpectedly at his easy acquiescence.

I broke the connection, not trusting myself to speak.

I took several deep breaths, slowly gaining control of my galloping emotions. There was no time for anything but the job at hand.

I swallowed hard and called William Robinson.

Mr. Robinson proved to be just as rigid as I expected, but he agreed to meet me for a late breakfast, and he didn't object when I asked if I could bring my financial advisor along. I didn't bother to explain he was also my boyfriend, or that he was technically my mother's financial advisor, not mine. I didn't have enough finances to need advice beyond "You can't afford it." And that I could do for myself for free.

I think my offer to pay for breakfast helped.

I called Wade back and told him to meet me at Franklin's in thirty minutes. It would give us a few minutes before Mr. Robinson arrived.

I reluctantly closed the laptop without looking at any of the files. I didn't want to leave the computer in the house, so I packed it into a carrying case and slung it over my shoulder.

The early summer morning was clear, the sky a pale blue with high, wispy clouds. Temptation beckoned, and I debated for about ten seconds before I opened the garage and unlocked the 'Vette.

It was way more car than I needed for the five-minute drive to Franklin's. I didn't care. I backed out of the garage with fifteen minutes to spare and a determination to make the most of my time.

The leather seat cradled me as I pulled onto the highway. Traffic was light. The engine growled softly, a promise of power waiting to be unleashed. The candy-apple red paint and chrome accents drew admiring looks from other drivers, the painstaking restoration a testament to the restoration team's pride and the owner's pocketbook.

The latter was a sham now, but when I'd cashed my first stock options it had been real; the car was tangible proof that I'd "made it." Even when Samurai Security was stolen from me and I fled San Francisco I'd held on to the Corvette. The car had carried me and all my worldly goods back to the Great North-wet. The simple act of rolling down the windows and letting it loose on the highway for a few minutes was a reminder that I had survived. The wind in my hair was invigorating, though I probably looked like I'd used an eggbeater instead of a comb.

I didn't care.

I turned around in a rest stop a few miles east of town and headed back. I pulled into Franklin's lot and found a safe parking spot between Wade's sensible hybrid sedan and a traffic divider. Driving a car with a fiberglass body meant being very careful where you parked.

I ran my fingers through my hair in an unsuccessful effort to make it behave. Wade spotted me and waved from a table in the back corner.

We were in the short lull between early-morning tourists headed up the mountain for the day and the after-church local crowd. The tables nearby were empty and I got the impression Wade had planned it that way.

I hugged Wade and sat down next to him, stowing the computer case under my chair. "Thanks for coming," I said. I waved the waitress away with the explanation that we were waiting for one more person. "Just coffee for now."

After she left I turned to Wade. "Tell me about this lawyer."

"Like I told you, we were in business school together. When we graduated he decided to try law school. Spent a summer as an intern in the Public Defender's office and discovered he liked trial work." He toyed with his silverware, fidgeting as he had the night before. "We keep in touch."

I reached over and put my hand over his. "Thank you,

Wade. You did me a huge favor by finding this guy. By the way, I probably ought to know his name."

"Oops! I knew I was forgetting something. It's David Young. He did call me back, by the way. It's all set for him to see your mother at one. He said he'd call when they're done."

I nodded. "Okay."

Wade gestured toward the computer case on the floor. "How come you're dragging a laptop around with you?"

I glanced around before I answered. "It's my mother's. I'm sure the sheriff would like to get his hands on it. I didn't want to leave it at home. Just in case." When I said it out loud, it sounded paranoid.

I laughed nervously. "I know how that sounds. But I found a folder named 'Veritas' on there. I think it's back-ups of Gregory's files."

Wade looked properly impressed. "He just left files sitting around on your mom's laptop?"

"They weren't exactly just sitting around," I admitted. "I had to do some poking around. A lot of poking around actually. I was up most of the night."

"I thought you were going to get some rest when we left."

I shook my head. "I wish. I knew there was something on the laptop and I didn't know how long I'd be able to work on it. I figured last night might be my only chance."

"So what did you find?"

"Nothing yet," I admitted. "Every time I try to look at the files I get interrupted. But once I talk to William Robinson I might have a better idea what it is I'm looking for."

"Speaking of Mr. Robinson," Wade said, "there's a guy up front. Looks like this might be our breakfast date."

William Robinson nodded at the hostess and headed for our table. "Ms. Neverall?" he said when he reached the table.

"Yes, I'm Georgiana Neverall. Are you Mr. Robinson?" I managed to keep the incredulity out of my voice. On the telephone, William Robinson had been precise to the point of rigidity. He sounded like a prissy little man who'd wear his shirts buttoned to the top and his hair precisely trimmed.

In person he was overweight and bearded, with a polo shirt a couple sizes too small. His dark eyes held a quick intelligence behind heavy-framed glasses.

I introduced Robinson to Wade, reminding him—and Wade—that Wade was there as my financial advisor. I wasn't sure why I felt the deception was necessary, but I didn't know who to trust, and even though Paula had introduced me to Robinson, how much did she really know about him?

The waitress returned and took our order. Apparently Mr. Robinson believed in a hearty breakfast—especially when someone else was picking up the tab. My stomach thought eggs and bacon would be good, but my wallet said oatmeal.

Oatmeal won.

"Mr. Robinson," I said once we were alone, "I appreciate your taking the time to come and talk to us. Ms. Ciccone tells me you're quite knowledgeable about wine?"

I swear the man simpered. His mouth pursed into a tiny rosebud and he cocked his head to one side. "I'm merely a student of enology, Ms. Neverall. A grateful recipient of the winemaker's gifts."

I kept my expression respectful, though it took an effort. False modesty never impressed me, especially when it was so blatant. "Ms. Ciccone did say you were well read in the field, Mr. Robinson." I smiled in what I hoped was a disarming way. "When I asked her if there was a wine expert in Pine Ridge, you're the one she thought of. Of course," I amended quickly, "she didn't tell me who you were until after she called you."

"Please, call me William." Robinson lifted the corners of his mouth in a tight-lipped imitation of a smile. "I like to think I have some knowledge, but I'm hardly an expert. I have so much to learn—more than I could hope to gain in a single lifetime."

Who really talked like this? Paula was absolutely right; the guy was definitely a character. I'd have used a stronger word.

"Do you know anything about investing in wine?" Wade went right to the point. "I understand that's become quite popular in recent years."

"Wine has always been considered something of an investment," William preached, clearly enjoying the chance to parade his knowledge. "There are several varieties that are simply undrinkable for ten years or more, and they improve with age. In order to experience the full mastery of the winemaker, you must be willing to wait, sometimes for decades. You must be willing to invest the time, to buy in *anticipation*, to have the patience to wait until the wine is ready."

He continued to expound on the topic for several minutes, while I waited patiently for him to reach a conclusion. An end didn't appear to be in sight. When William paused for breath Wade slid into the second of silence.

"Do the wines increase in value during that time?" he asked, trying to pull William's diatribe back to the questions we needed answered.

William's pedantic display of knowledge disappeared, replaced by scorn and derision. "What you really want to know is whether it increases in price, correct?" he sneered. "As though that's the measure of a wine's value. The wine's value increases, yes, and often the price reflects that. But a true enophile doesn't care how much or how little a bottle costs. They only care about what is inside. Does the bouquet entice you to sip? Does it please the tongue? Is the flavor as expected? Price is nothing compared to the pleasure a good wine can provide."

"That makes sense," I said. "But aren't there people that speculate in wine? I've heard people talk about filling their wine cellar and they say it's a good investment, as if it's going to increase in"—I almost said *value*, but I stopped myself— "price and they'll make a profit reselling it."

William snorted and looked down his nose. "Yes, there

are people like that. I am not one of them. They buy wine as though it were a barrel of oil or a share of stock. To them it is only a thing to buy and sell.

"I buy wine to drink." He shoveled a bite of eggs and potatoes into his mouth. He chewed so hard his jaw clicked with each bite and his face reddened. The intensity of his feelings was very clear.

"Oh, no," I said. "We don't want to invest like that, and I certainly didn't mean to imply you did. Heavens, no! We're just looking into some existing investments, trying to find the parties involved. We thought you might know where we should look, who the reputable dealers are, that sort of thing."

The clicking eased and the angry glow receded from his face. His expression turned thoughtful. "There are a few wine merchants who might be able to help. A lot of higher-end wine is sold at auction, however. Those might not be so easy to trace."

Wade stepped back in. "Have you heard about a local group of investors, William? I understand someone put together a group several months back. I believe it was called Veritas."

"I was approached," he said. "I declined the invitation. It may be the same group, it may not. When I realized what they planned to do, I refused to have anything to do with their so-called investment group. I never knew what they chose to call themselves."

"But it might have been them?" I asked.

"Possibly."

"Who approached you?" Wade asked.

William didn't hesitate. "Phil Wilson, the car dealer. That's the only name I know for sure."

Phil Wilson was a local institution. He'd owned a string of auto dealerships on the eastern edge of Portland before he retired to a twenty-room "cabin" on the edge of Pine Ridge. His sons ran the dealerships but Phil was still the spokesman for the Wilson Auto Group, with his picture at the top of the display ads in the Saturday classifieds and his booming voice proclaiming, "If you don't come see me, I can't save you money" on late night TV.

Phil Wilson seemed a bit crude next to the too-smooth image of Gregory Whitlock, but they were both self-made men who seemed to have a lot of money. It that respect they were a perfect fit.

"Did Mr. Wilson give you any indication who they were buying from?"

William swabbed his plate with the last bite of toast as he considered the question. He popped the toast into his mouth and shook his head.

"No. I got the impression they hadn't actually bought anything yet when he talked to me. In fact, he asked me for recommendations as though they were just getting started. I didn't pay a lot of attention, to tell the truth. I made it clear I thought it was a dreadful idea, and dismissed the scheme from my mind. I hadn't thought about it since." He nodded in my direction. "At least not until your friend the librarian called me."

William pulled a business card from his wallet and handed it to me. "My office number is on there, if you think of any other questions."

I glanced at the card before I put it in my pocket. He was the payroll department manager for a truck manufacturing plant in Portland. It seemed an odd place for a connoisseur of fine wine. Then again, you didn't expect to find a Caltech computer scientist under a sink.

William was on his feet, shrugging into his jacket, when he snapped his fingers and looked at me. "You might try Vendage in the Pearl. I gave Phil Wilson their card."

Our check arrived and I dutifully hauled out my credit card. It hadn't been a cheap meal, thanks to William's appetite, but it had given me the next link in the chain. Now I needed to talk to Phil Wilson and ask him about Veritas.

Easier said than done.

chapter 20

We left Franklin's in separate cars with the same destination: Wade's office. His friend David Young was meeting with my mother and he had promised to call us as soon as they were through.

I stopped at the house to change cars and let the dogs out. Much as I loved driving the 'Vette, I didn't want to park it on Main Street on Sunday afternoon and advertise my presence at Wade's office.

The Beetle was a little more discreet.

Wade left the door unlocked for me. He was at his desk with a mound of file folders, several of them bulging with computer printouts. He already had his computer on and was typing rapidly.

"Behold the paperless office," he joked. "Weren't you computer types supposed to save us from all this?" He gestured toward the piles on the desk, nearly toppling one precarious stack.

"And weren't you accountant types supposed to give up your paper files and trust the electronic ones?" I shot back. I knew Wade could have cut the paper files in half, or more, if he was willing to trust the electronic backups he made with regularity.

Instead he kept paper and electronic copies of all his files, which threatened to overwhelm his tiny storefront office. He was constantly culling his files and putting boxes into the bulging storage unit he maintained nearby.

Judging from the stacks of cartons lining the back wall it was about time for another storage run. And probably time to rent another unit.

He registered the laptop case slung over my shoulder and waved me toward his clerk's desk. "Use Karen's desk if you want," he said. "You have the passwords for the wireless if you need it."

"Thanks." I sat down, booted up Mom's laptop, and went back to work on the Veritas folder. I was determined to find out what was in there.

The spreadsheets were easy. In the locked folder Gregory had obviously assumed the files were safe and there were no passwords or locks on the files themselves.

The contents, on the other hand, were going to take some translation.

"Wade?"

"Um-hmm?" Wade looked up, startled. He had been deeply engrossed in his papers, and it was as if he had forgotten I was there.

"Can you take a look at this with me? I have no idea what some of these fields might mean."

Wade rolled his chair over to where I sat and peered at the laptop screen over my shoulder. Maybe Gregory knew what the various rows and columns meant, but his labels were cryptic to the point of being indecipherable, though some could be guessed from the content.

I connected to Wade's wireless network and negotiated the security system so I could search wine terminology.

Wade was one of the few people in Pine Ridge that didn't need the Samurai Security standard lecture. Everything he did was hidden behind firewalls and password protected.

Like I said, he took his clients' privacy seriously.

Which was why I was startled when he dropped a file folder on my desk.

I glanced at the tab and did a double take. "Whitlock,

Gregory" was printed on the file tab in Wade's precise block lettering.

Wade put his palm down on the folder, holding it against the desktop. "You said your mother made you read the prenup agreement. Prove it. Tell me what you know about Whitlock's finances."

It took me several minutes to remember and piece together all the things I had read in Mom and Gregory's prenuptial agreement. There were houses and cars and rental property—I'd been surprised to learn Mom had acquired several small houses around town and grateful I hadn't ended up with her for a landlord.

Gregory had Whitlock Estates, of course, and he also had interests in a couple commercial developments. There had been a long list of personal property, including some art and collectibles that had surprised me. They shouldn't have; they were all pieces acquired with an eye to appreciation in price, not appreciation of aesthetics.

He had included the purchase price of all the major pieces and their current appraisals. Either he was very good at picking pieces that increased in value, or he regularly pruned anything whose market value wasn't growing fast enough. I suspected the latter. In Gregory's world, everything was expected to turn a profit.

Mom's financial acumen had caught me by surprise. She had allowed my father to handle the finances when he was alive and it had nearly bankrupted her when he died. In the years since, she had learned a lot about money and it showed clearly in her part of the prenup.

I said as much to Wade.

"She's a very smart woman, Georgie. Don't underestimate what your mother is capable of when she puts her mind to it."

He lifted his hand from the file and flipped the folder open. "I don't think there's anything in here you don't already know," he said. "But let's go through it and see if there's something we missed."

The stack of receipts and statements in the folder was huge, and we each took a portion of it and began flipping through the pages. I finished my stack and reached for another handful, and Wade did the same.

I was near the bottom of the second stack when I found the first clue. On a credit card statement from early in the spring there was a charge for seven thousand dollars to Vendage, the wine merchant William Robinson had told us about.

I held it out to Wade. "Look." My hand shook with nervous excitement, making the paper tremble. "Maybe this will help."

Wade took the paper from me. "Right there." I pointed to the line. "He used his own credit card."

Wade studied the line for a minute, then scooted over to look at the screen of the laptop where the enigmatic spreadsheet was still displayed.

He used the computer to find the telephone number for Vendage and reached for the phone on Karen's desk.

I listened to Wade's end of the conversation with growing astonishment.

"Good afternoon, Marie. This is Wade Montgomery. I'm Gregory Whitlock's accountant. I'm working on some reports this afternoon and I had a question." He paused, then chuckled. "Yeah, it's a horrible day to be cooped up inside, especially on a Sunday. But if I don't finish up these Whitlock reports I'll have worse problems than missing a day of sunshine."

His voice dropped into a conspiratorial softness. "Thing is, Marie, I have a couple invoices here that I'm having a problem with and I was hoping maybe you could help me out."

He waited. All I could hear from the other end was the hesitant squeak of the woman's voice.

"Oh, no! I have all the credit card information. You wouldn't have to tell me anything like that. I just need to know exactly what was purchased."

There was more squeaking. "Of course," Wade said soothingly. "I wouldn't expect you to do that. Just verify the quantities so I can post this to the right place."

He chuckled apologetically. "You know how we accountants can be. I can call back tomorrow if I have to, but I'd really like to be able to get this right the first time."

Wade sat very still. After a long moment, he read off the date and amount of the charges. "Can you find that invoice?" he asked.

We waited silently for several minutes, and our patience was rewarded when Wade's new friend returned with the details of the purchase: two cases of Bordeaux. She gave Wade the vineyard and the year and said Mr. Whitlock had received his standard discount.

Wade thanked Marie, and promised to stop and see her the next time he was in the area.

I stared at him in disbelief as he hung up.

"You lied to her!"

"I did not. I will stop and see her the next time I get to the Pearl District." There was a twinkle in his eye. "I just didn't tell her I never go to the Pearl. Not my style."

With the information from the invoice, we were able to locate the line in the spreadsheet that represented the two cases of Bordeaux. It gave us a clue to begin decoding the other entries.

Wade's office phone rang and he reached to pick it up. I kept working on the spreadsheet. When he hung up, he told me it had been David Young, the attorney. He was on his way over.

I would have to close the file and put away the computer before Young got there. He was Mom's attorney, not mine, and I didn't think it would be a good idea for him to know I had the laptop.

"Before I close this thing, I want you to take a look at something," I said.

I pointed to a column and started scrolling down the

page. "If this is the number of bottles—which we think it is, based on that one invoice—then Gregory had a couple hundred cases of wine."

I tried to envision what two hundred cases of wine would look like. "Do you think he's got that stashed in his house?" I asked Wade. "Is his wine cellar anywhere near that big?"

I did some quick mental math as I shut down the computer. "Even if they're only a hundred bucks a pop, like the ones from Vendage, that's close to a quarter million dollars. That's a lot of money to have sitting in the wine cellar of an empty house."

"There's a security system," Wade said. "He told me about it when they started construction. We were working on the insurance coverage for the house and it made a big difference in his premiums. He paid a small fortune for it, but now I begin to understand why. It wasn't just his investment in Veritas that was at stake."

A late-model BMW pulled up in front of the office. The driver climbed out and walked toward the door.

I shoved the computer case under the desk. The modesty panel hid it from prying eyes. I'd get back to the e-mail files later.

Wade greeted David Young warmly.

Young was nothing like I expected. Wade was six feet tall, give or take, but Young towered over him. He had to be at least six five or six, and broad. Not fat, just big. Wide shoulders and a barrel chest were barely contained by his custom-tailored charcoal suit. For a man his size you didn't get a fit like that off the rack.

David Young stuck out a huge hand. "Hi, I'm David. Dave to my friends. You must be Georgiana." He grinned. "You have your mother's eyes."

I felt a blush creep up my neck and spread across my face. My mother always insisted I looked like my father's side of the family, probably because I didn't bother with the clothes and makeup that were her trademarks. It felt funny to have someone say I looked like her in any way.

"I mean that as a compliment," David said. "She's an attractive woman."

I resisted the impulse to tell him he only thought that because he didn't know her very well. He'd find out for himself soon enough.

We settled around Wade's desk, with Dave in the visitor's chair and me in Karen's borrowed secretarial chair.

Dave didn't waste time. "I talked to your mother," he said. "She agreed to have me represent her, with the understanding that I would have the backing of a senior member of the firm if this goes to trial."

My face must have shown the dismay I felt. Wasn't Mom's lawyer supposed to avoid going to trial?

"It won't," Dave assured me. "They can't make this stick. I don't know Vernon personally, but I know his type. There were a lot of them in the prosecutor's office when I was on the other side. Young and ambitious. They wait for a case that will get them noticed so they can either move up the ladder or get an offer in the private sector."

That didn't make me feel any better. "So this guy is ambitious and he sees Mom as a way to make a name for himself. That doesn't exactly build my confidence, Dave."

"I understand your concern, Ms. Neverall. Believe me, it isn't going to happen." He handed Wade a note. "Mrs. Neverall said you would be able to access funds for her retainer."

Wade looked at the paper and back to Dave. "Can I write you a check?"

Dave nodded.

Wade wrote the check and returned the checkbook to his safe.

Dave stuck it in his pocket without looking. "My client," he said formally, "has instructed me to share with you whatever I feel is appropriate. That doesn't mean I am going to tell you everything she says, or everything we talk about. Because I represent Sandra, and I do not represent

either of you, the things we talk about do not fall under
attorney-client privilege. You could be forced to testify in
court about our conversations."

Dave looked from Wade to me, and back again. "You
both understand that?"

We nodded.

"Just keep that in mind if I tell you I can't tell you
something."

Was I good with that? I wasn't sure. There probably *were*
things I didn't want to know.

I got the answer to that quicker than I could have imagined.

There were definitely things I didn't want to know. Like
exactly how Gregory died.

"He was stabbed," Dave told us. "With a knife the police believe came from Sandra's kitchen. I don't have all
the details as yet, but apparently he was stabbed in the
house and shoved through the access hatch into the crawl
space." He nodded to me. "Where you found him."

"Access hatch?" My voice sounded far away. It echoed
in my head like a bad cell phone connection.

"In the hallway," Dave replied. "That's as much as I was
able to get immediately. I'll know more after the preliminary hearing."

"Is that the one tomorrow?" I asked. "Do we know what
time?"

I realized I was going to have to call Barry and arrange
for time off. He'd give me whatever I needed, but I hated
to lose the hours if I didn't have to.

Dave told me I didn't need to be at the hearing. I battled
with some serious guilt for a few minutes, but he convinced
me there wasn't anything I could do and I wouldn't get to
talk to Mom.

I tried to pay attention as Dave explained how the legal
process would play out over the next few days and weeks.
He told us the police had finished their search of Gregory's
house and office, but Mom's house was still restricted.

Even if she could get bail, she couldn't go home yet.

That last fact caught my attention. "Do you think she'll be allowed to post bail?"

Dave shook his head. "I expect Vernon to oppose bail, and without knowing who the judge is . . ."

It was one of those good news/bad news situations.

The good news was I didn't have Mom taking over my house. The bad news was she had to stay in jail.

And the worse news was I had to somehow fix that.

Clamps and a rubber blanket should stop most leaks for several months. Keep some clamps sized to fit your pipes and a sheet of rubber on hand for emergencies. If you don't have a clamp, you can still fix a small leak *temporarily* in an emergency by plugging it with a pencil point. Sharpen a pencil, push it into the leak, and break the point off in place. But it's important to get the problem fixed the correct way as soon as it is practical.

—A Plumber's Tip from Georgiana Neverall

chapter 21

Although "contortionist" is not included in the job description for a plumber, it's a useful skill. Crawl spaces are often tight and filled with ducts, pipes, joists, and footings. The cabinets under most sinks are cramped, with doors that don't open fully or frames that restrict access.

Answering a cell phone while under a sink calls for the flexibility of a gymnast. It also helps if you're the size of an underweight twelve-year-old. Neither one describes me.

By the time I got out from under the island sink in Astrid McComb's new kitchen the call had gone to voice mail. I waited, staring out the window at the sunlit woods surrounding the castle, for the caller to leave a message. It had to be Dave with the results of Mom's preliminary hearing.

It wasn't.

"Ms. Neverall, this is William Robinson calling. You wanted to know about the Veritas group. I heard from a wine merchant I know about some interesting vintages being auctioned tonight. Wolfe-Bowers Auction House in Portland is mounting the sale. Perhaps they will be able to offer you some information."

The message ended, and I wondered why he had taken the time to call. He'd certainly left me with the impression he wanted nothing to do with our investigation.

On the other hand, maybe he hoped I would cause trouble for Veritas, since he had clearly disliked them.

Either way, I needed to find out about the auction. Quickly.

I called Wade's office and asked him if he had plans for the evening.

"There's a City Council meeting starting at six," he said. "I'm afraid it might run late."

He was apologetic, but he had run for Councilman and he took the responsibility very seriously. He couldn't skip the meeting, even for me.

I respected his dedication and sense of responsibility. Really, I did.

I just wished it didn't have to interfere with my investigation of Veritas.

Sue volunteered to find out about the sale at Wolfe-Bowers, much to my relief. She could surf the Web and make phone calls between customers at Doggy Day Spa—I had to get back under the sink.

But Sue had plans with Fred for the evening, and even though she offered to cancel them and go with me I told her no.

Our friendship got in the way of our romantic relationships a little too often as it was and I'd already given Sue enough grief over Fred.

My next call was to Paula. I caught her at the library and explained the situation. She couldn't care less about the wine itself, but the outing appealed to her—as did the investigation.

"Sounds like fun, Georgie! Megan's working on a school project with her dad tonight. They can just call Garibaldi's for pizza like they always do when I'm not home for dinner." She laughed. "They don't think I know, but I do."

I promised to pick her up, and crawled back under the sink. I still had a job to do.

I finished the sink in the island and went in search of the cabinet crew. They were supposed to have the granite countertop and bowl installed and ready for me to connect.

They didn't and they told me it wouldn't be ready until morning. Neither would the fixtures in the master bathroom. For now, the plumbing work was at a standstill.

Barry didn't have another assignment for me when I called him, but he said he'd talked to Paula about our plans for the evening.

"Thanks for asking her, Georgie. She loves stuff like this."

"And you don't." It wasn't a question. Barry was a small-town, blue-collar kind of guy. His idea of an upscale wine was one that came with a cork instead of a screw top, and he'd still rather have a beer than either one.

"I'm heading home then, Bear." It was a nickname that fit him, though I didn't use it very often. After all, he was my boss, even though sometimes he felt like the older brother I never had.

Especially when I was planning a girls' night out with his wife.

I was willing to bet Paula hadn't told him the real reason we were going to the auction, either. He tended to be a rather old-fashioned and protective when it came to his wife—and to his female employees.

Even the ones with martial-arts training.

I still hadn't heard from Dave Young, and it was beginning to worry me. What if something went wrong with Mom's hearing?

I pulled the Beetle to the curb in front of Wade's office. Maybe he had heard something.

No such luck.

"Dave said he'd call, Georgie, and he will. He's a very reliable guy."

"How can you be sure?" I was whining and I knew it. Like Daisy, I didn't do "stay" very well, and the waiting was driving me nuts.

"I've known him a lot of years, and we've worked on several community projects together. Believe me, when Dave Young says he'll do something, he does it." Wade glanced from me to his cluttered desktop and back. His meaning was clear. He had work to do.

"Karen's at the doctor's this afternoon," he said. "If you want to wait here, you can use her desk."

It was a better idea than sitting at home, stewing.

I dragged the laptop into the office and set to work on the Veritas files. I still hadn't had time to decipher Gregory's e-mail. The longer it went unread, the more convinced I became that I would find all the answers there.

When Dave's call finally came, it was anticlimactic. Mom had been arraigned, bail was set at a million dollars, and she was taken back to her cell.

Dave had been in a meeting with the Deputy Prosecutor, looking for a way to get the bail reduced. Vernon had been adamant; he thought Sandra Neverall committed a murder and he wanted her kept in jail. He was angry that the judge had considered bail at all.

All Mom's properties together wouldn't cover a million dollars, and a bond would cost ten percent of that amount. If she was going to get out of jail, we had to come up with one hundred thousand dollars.

Or we had to find the real killer.

chapter 22

I left Wade's office and headed home. I had to pick up Paula in an hour for the trip into Portland, but my heart wasn't in it.

There was no way to get my mother out of jail, even temporarily, without catching the real murderer.

I felt a serious pity party coming on. To combat it, I put the dogs on their leashes and allowed the three of us a thirty-minute walk. The sun was still warm, and there were many new smells to check out since we hadn't been for a walk in several days.

Daisy and Buddha would have happily kept going for several hours, sniffing each tree and burrowing into each bush seeking out the messages left by other dogs. I, on the other hand, had a date to keep.

By the time we turned for home my spirits had lifted a little. I was going out for the evening with a good friend. A wine auction might not have been my first choice of entertainment, but it was something new and different, and it promised the opportunity for lots of people-watching.

And it might bring me one step closer to Gregory's killer and Mom's freedom.

I showered and faced the dilemma of what to wear. Years earlier I'd had a closet full of designer and business wear and expensive shoes. Now I dug in the back of Mom's closet—it had been mine just a few days ago—and found a classic little black dress. I tossed a brocade jacket on top to fend off the evening chill and found my black pumps.

Lacking pockets, I tossed the bare necessities into a small shoulder bag. I was ready to go.

As I locked the door behind me, I looked at the keys. Keys to my house, to Mom's house, Beetle keys, a padlock key for my toolbox, and the Corvette key.

Why not? It was a night out.

I opened the garage door and slid into the driver's seat. The engine roared to life. I backed into the street, goosed the accelerator, and eased out the clutch, feeling the power of nearly four hundred horses at my disposal.

I smiled for the first time in days as I drove the couple miles to Barry and Paula's house. Somehow I always felt like the queen of the world when I was behind the wheel of my beloved vintage Corvette.

Paula must have been waiting by the door. She came hurrying down the walk as soon as I pulled up. Barry stood in the doorway and waved to us as we pulled away.

"Wow!" Paula fastened her seat belt. "I wasn't expecting you to bring the 'Vette! This just gets better by the minute."

On the drive in I filled Paula in on my plans for the evening.

She'd never been to a wine auction, either, but she'd spent the afternoon reading up on the subject. She even, she reported proudly, had searched Google for wine auction information.

When I first came back to Pine Ridge, Paula had barely been able to turn on her computer to log books in and out at the library. Now, with the occasional help of her secret consultant—namely me—she kept the two public terminals connected and humming along, and she was learning to use the electronic tools at her disposal.

After Blake Weston's murder, a lot more people were aware of my computer skills and I found myself fielding calls for help with increasing frequency. Sometimes it was a friend or a coworker, and I tried to do what I could to bail them out.

In a town the size of Pine Ridge there was no such thing as a complete stranger, but there were lots of people who were acquaintances, not friends. And lately I'd been getting calls from some of those people, too. My reputation was beginning to spread and I didn't know what to do about it. It was a problem I had to address. Soon.

But right now, I had bigger fish to fry.

We pulled up in front of the simple and elegant brick building and climbed out. I swallowed hard and handed my keys to the valet. Knowing I wouldn't have to park on the street was comforting. Letting someone else drive my toy was nerve-wracking.

Inside the door a registration table stood along one wall. Behind it a young man with spiky hair greeted most of the buyers by name. The bidders carried their own catalogs, already well thumbed and dog-eared. They signed a register, took a paddle with a number, and moved into the main room.

We inched along, moving closer to Mr. Spiky Hair.

As we got to the front of the line, Paula stepped in front of me and gave Spiky Hair a dazzling smile. "Need to register," she said, "decided to come at the last minute."

She signed the register and gave the guy a flash of her driver's license. She took the paddle and the catalog he offered her, and returned him another smile.

I stepped forward, but Paula took me by the arm and pulled me away. "We're together," she said as she dragged me toward the door.

"No need to have your name in the register," she whispered.

Paula had seen too many spy movies.

The large room hummed with muted conversations as the bidders conferred with one another and consulted their catalogs. I caught a glimpse of a couple catalogs marked with multiple colors and indecipherable codes. These people took this very seriously.

I looked around the room, taking in the crowd. They were a mix of ages and sizes with one thing in common: money. Some of it was understated, some of it was flaunted, but it was definitely there.

Good thing I'd brought the 'Vette. At least we had some camouflage.

At the front of the room I spotted Phil Wilson. He had less hair and more pounds than in his TV ads, but there was no mistaking the voice that had boomed out on every commercial break. While most people talked in low voices sort of like they were in church, Wilson's volume control was set just a little shy of deafening.

He commented to his companion, a woman young enough to be his daughter and anorexic enough to be a model, on several lots that he thought he should bid on. Mostly he seemed concerned with the prices, dismissing anything without a high reserve. If the seller didn't think it was worth a minimum, how good could it be?

We drifted closer to Wilson, listening to his nonstop commentary. Paula said softly that he obviously didn't know a thing about wine. With a single afternoon of computer research, a new skill she delighted in showing off, she could see several errors in Wilson's thinking.

"The man wouldn't know a vintage port from a bottle of Mad Dog," she said in an indignant whisper.

Still, he was the only link we had to Veritas, and I wanted to talk to him if I could. From the way Model-Girl clung to his arm like he was a prize catch, I wasn't sure we would be allowed close.

We moved toward a couple chairs at a table next to Wilson. Several other bidders were beginning to take their seats as the official starting time approached.

Just then Wilson turned to survey the room. His gaze raked the assembled group, and I caught a glimpse of the shrewd intelligence that had kept him on top of the used-car game for forty years.

He might be a bombastic jerk who was ignorant about wine, but he wasn't stupid.

In that moment he climbed high up my suspect list.

Well, it wasn't much of a list. In fact, right now it consisted of only Phil Wilson, which pretty much guaranteed him the top spot. But he did seem to deserve it.

His eyes lit on Paula and a momentary confusion knotted his brow. Within seconds he identified her and extended a hand. "Mrs. Hickey! How good to see you. I didn't know you were a wine aficionado."

He turned to the woman on his arm. "Heather, this is Mrs. Hickey. Her husband's a contractor in Pine Ridge. I sold him a couple rigs, and he did some work for me on the cabin."

I managed to control my impulse to laugh. His so-called cabin had at least six bedrooms, a private theater, and three kitchens, including one on the flagstone terrace. I hadn't been on the crew, but I knew Barry had installed solid-brass fixtures, steam showers, and jetted tubs in all four bathrooms, and put in natural gas heating units on the various decks.

Barry referred to it as the Hawaiian vacation cabin, since it had paid for an anniversary trip to the Islands.

Paula kept a rigid smile on her face. She wasn't Mrs. Hickey, she was Ms. Ciccone, but this guy clearly didn't know that. I had to give her credit; she didn't try to correct him. She was making the sacrifice for the sake of my investigation and I appreciated her restraint.

Paula introduced me as an associate of her husband, and laughed merrily, as though Phil Wilson was actually charming. "Hardly an aficionado," she said. "Georgiana and I just started learning about wine, and we thought the opportunity to see a real live auction was too good to pass up."

I smiled and shook the hand he extended toward me. "Glad to meet you," he said. "You work with Barry, huh? Great guy. Great guy! You ever need a car, you come down to the dealership. Tell my boy I said he should take good care of you."

I didn't mention that I drove a car worth more than

anything on his lot and had no intention of replacing it, though I was tempted.

"Yes," I gushed. "Barry's a great guy. It was really sweet of him to let me steal his wife for the evening."

I think Paula had an elbow ready to dig into my ribs, but I moved a step closer to Wilson and she couldn't reach me.

"I heard about your cabin," I continued. "Someone told me you had a great wine cellar."

Wilson launched into a long-winded explanation of his wine cellar and his collection. Every sentence contained a reference to how much one thing or another cost.

I was beginning to sympathize with William's assessment of the man.

"Philly," Heather whined at his elbow. She had had enough of the conversation, and of the two of us. "Philly, I need some champagne."

I bit my tongue. The name was actually appropriate. He was "cheesy" enough.

He didn't move. Just dug into a pocket and stuffed a wad of bills in her hand. "Go find yourself some bubbly, girl. But hurry your sweet little self back here quick. This thing's about to start."

He waved her away with supreme confidence she'd return. I doubted it was misplaced. She looked like the kind who always came back to the source of a wad of bills.

"Sweet kid," he said, ogling her backside as she sashayed away.

"Now if you girls want to sit right here with us"—he motioned at a couple of seats at his table—"I'd be glad to give you a few pointers."

"Oh, no." Paula sounded genuinely alarmed.

I didn't blame her. The idea of spending the rest of the evening in the company of this windbag gave me a severe pain.

"We couldn't impose on you," she said. "Although I did have a question . . ."

"It's no imposition, I assure you." He smiled, his mouth drawing into an almost sneer of superiority. "Ask away."

"I've been hearing about a wine group in Pine Ridge," she said. "I think it was called Veritas."

I watched Wilson closely when she said the name. I thought I saw the jolly persona slip for a split second, but Heather returned with two glasses of champagne at that moment, and I couldn't be sure of what I'd seen. Maybe he just wasn't that happy to have her back.

She handed a glass to Wilson and tapped her glass against his. "Cheers," she said and took a big sip. She was staking her claim and making sure we knew we were most definitely not welcome to join them.

Paula and I both moved back a step, but Wilson wasn't going to let his date run us off that easily.

"Never heard of them, but I'll keep an ear out and let you know if I do." He shook his head. "Small town for any kind of wine investors."

Paula hadn't said anything about investors. I wondered if Wilson's denial was for the sake of his companion, or if there was a darker reason.

Wilson quickly shifted back into salesman mode, as though anxious to put the discussion of Veritas behind him.

"You sure I can't get you to come down and look at a car?" He fished in his pocket for a business card, grabbed my hand, and pressed it into my palm. "Make you a good deal on your trade-in, too."

"'Fraid not." I gave him my sweetest smile. "I have a vintage Corvette. No way am I trading him in on anything."

The intelligence flashed in his eyes again, and I could almost see the gears turning as he regarded me. I wasn't what he had originally thought.

"A woman who appreciates the classics." There was a hint of something in his voice. Once upon a time, I was sure, this man had loved cars. All cars. Not just the ones that represented money in the bank.

But not anymore.

"If you ever change your mind, you bring it to me," he said. "We'll treat you right."

I believed that even less than I believed the other things he'd told me.

Paula and I made polite excuses and moved away from Philly and Heather. They made a perfect couple, and we left them to it.

I felt like I needed a shower after just a few minutes in the man's presence, and judging from Paula's expression, she did, too.

"Geor-gee," she whined, her voice too soft to carry, "I need some champagne."

I looked at her and we broke into giggles.

The auctioneer took the podium and rapped a polished wooden gavel against the top of the podium. Conversation died, and the few people who were standing quickly found seats.

I moved to the back of the room, in order to have a better view, and Paula moved with me. From our vantage point against the wall we were able to watch everyone.

The auctioneer recited a list of rules that took several minutes. Many of them boiled down to "If you don't want to buy it, don't bid on it." People around the room nodded and looked solemn. A few even seemed to be mouthing the words with him, as if they knew them by heart.

This was serious business to the buyers and the auctioneers.

It was completely unlike the unclaimed storage auctions at the Pine Ridge Stor-It-Urself. That was the only auction I'd ever been to.

The people, though, were familiar types. I'd met people like them when we were raising venture capital for Samurai Security. I knew how to adopt the protective coloring necessary to move in this crowd.

We watched in silence for more than an hour, as each lot was brought out, lovingly described, and then sold to the highest bidder. Wilson's bidding followed a pattern. He only bought expensive cases.

The auctioneer called a break after about ninety minutes. He had been sipping regularly from a water bottle as he worked his spiel, but his voice was beginning to thicken and sound scratchy the last few minutes before he stopped. "Fifteen minutes," he announced as he left the stage.

People moved slowly in all directions—some to the restrooms, some to the refreshment table, some formed small clots of conversation, and a few headed for the exits.

I tried to watch Wilson, to see who he might talk to in the intermission. A large man stopped directly in my line of sight, and all I could see was a broad expanse of dark wool. When he stepped away, Wilson was no longer in sight.

I scanned the crowd, and finally spotted him—with Heather clinging to his arm as though he might float away at any moment. Wilson was deep in conversation with a man who looked vaguely familiar.

I nudged Paula. "Who's that talking to Wilson?"

She looked in the direction I indicated. "That's Taylor Parkson. Has a weekend place in Pine Ridge. Do you think he's part of Veritas?"

I shook my head. "Wish I knew. Don't think I've ever met him, but he looked kind of familiar. Maybe I've seen him around town."

"Could be," Paula answered. "He lives in Portland and he travels a lot, but he comes out every month or two for a weekend." She sighed. "Must be nice to be able to afford a house you only use a few days every other month."

"Yeah." I didn't tell her how close I'd come to being one of those people, too busy to enjoy what they had.

We watched as the two men exchanged handshakes. They both smiled politely, the way people do when they run into someone they don't know well.

The whole encounter only lasted a minute or two before Parkson nodded and moved on. He had barely turned his back when another man approached Wilson.

My mouth formed a little O of surprise and I turned to Paula. "Isn't that William?" I asked. "Did you know he was here?"

She shook her head, glancing over to confirm what we had both seen. "It's him, all right, but I'd swear he wasn't here when the auction started."

The two men moved back toward a corner of the room, like they were seeking a private spot for their huddled conversation. William kept his back to the room, and Phil Wilson kept glancing around as if he thought someone might be trying to eavesdrop.

"What can that be about?" Paula asked the question that was in the front of my mind.

"I'm not sure," I answered. "William sure gave me the impression that he didn't like Phil Wilson and he said he turned down an invitation to be part of their investment group. So if Wilson is part of Veritas, why is William Robinson having such an intense private conversation with him? At a wine auction?" I shook my head. "It doesn't make sense."

There were only a few minutes of the break left. We made our way to the refreshment table and each got a bottle of water. They had several wines available by the glass, but I passed. "I'm the designated driver," I joked to the girl in the caterer's uniform behind the table.

"Good for you!" she said, giving me a perky smile. "Wouldn't want to have to card you."

Given that the only thing being sold tonight was alcohol, it hardly seemed likely the caterers were checking ID, but she was trying to be friendly. I smiled and dropped a buck in the tip tray.

"Thanks," I said, lifting the bottle in a tiny salute as I walked away.

Paula and I went back to our places along the rear wall as the buyers began to drift back into their seats. There were a few chairs left empty by early departures, and I noticed William Robinson take a seat at the far left side. No one sat next to him.

The auctioneer returned to the stage and lifted his gavel. Within the first few minutes it was clear we were into more expensive lots. A couple bottles went for hundreds of dollars, and several cases were north of a hundred bucks per bottle.

When the first bottle crossed the four-figure mark, Paula gasped. Fortunately we were alone in the back of the room so no one heard her but me.

"Can you imagine," she whispered, "*drinking* a bottle of wine that cost that much?"

I had to admit it surprised me, too. I'd heard stories on the news about million-dollar bottles, but it was far different to watch someone actually bid, even at a thousand-dollar level. Especially someone you knew.

At the front of the room, Phil Wilson's paddle punched the air like a triumphant fist. I had the distinct impression that the people at the nearby tables pulled away from his outburst. It looked like Wilson had violated some auction etiquette rule that hadn't been on the list the auctioneer read.

The next-to-last lot was presented about half an hour later. Wilson had paid top dollar for a couple more cases. I could imagine him bragging to his golf buddies at the country club about how much he had spent. I wondered uncharitably how much he spent on Heather, and if he bragged about that, too.

This lot was three bottles of Burgundy, and it was instantly clear that William wanted the bottles. His posture went from relaxed to alert, and his eyes darted around the room as though assessing the competition.

A few more people had drifted out as it got later, but the remaining buyers were treated to an actual bidding war between William Robinson and Phil Wilson; a battle between the connoisseur and the cowboy.

The bidding rose quickly, then slowed. Robinson hesitated several times before bidding, and you could see him muttering to himself before each bid. I couldn't actually read his lips, but I imagined him saying, "One more bid. Just one more bid, and I quit."

Wilson won of course. Not surprising, considering he had way more money than sense. I ignored his victory antics and concentrated on William's reaction. He was obviously unhappy and disappointed. As soon as the auctioneer brought the gavel down for the last time, William reached for his coat draped across the empty chair next to him.

Before Wilson had finished celebrating, William was headed out the door.

chapter 23

The last lot was anticlimactic. Wilson wasn't interested and he created a minor disruption when he grabbed Heather and headed for the door. He paused just long enough to tell Spiky Hair to "make the usual arrangements" for payment and delivery.

Paula and I took our time. We watched how the other buyers went through the protocol of paying for their purchases and arranging delivery. Some of them had come prepared, and auction staff members helped them load carts or bags with their purchases.

The line for the parking valets began to grow. Paula drew my attention to a discreet sign to one side of the valet stand, "Vehicle Only, No Merchandise."

There was no one in the line.

It still took a few minutes for the Corvette to appear, as I watched a steady stream of Land Rovers and upscale SUVs pull to the curb to accept their cargo.

A young man in a valet uniform handed me the keys and I slipped a bill into his palm. "I feel like I ought to tip you." He grinned. "Driving that beauty is the most fun I've had all night."

I grinned back. That Corvette made me feel that way, too.

We pulled away from the curb and I pointed the 'Vette

toward the freeway. It was late and I was anxious to get home.

"Do you believe that girl?" Paula asked with undisguised glee.

"Heather?" I said.

"Cheers." Paula mimicked Heather perfectly, and I started giggling as I made the turn into the on-ramp.

Beside me, Paula's laughter welled up. "And did you see the way the people around them kept moving back?"

I accelerated into the light traffic and headed out of Portland. This late, the drive should only take fifteen or twenty minutes max. I might even get home early enough to spend some time combing through Gregory's e-mail files I still hadn't unlocked.

Paula had clearly enjoyed the evening. We compared notes on the people we'd seen, laughed at Phil Wilson's antics, and speculated on exactly what was going on between Phil Wilson and William Robinson.

"What was that bidding war all about?" Paula wondered aloud.

I shrugged and downshifted for our off-ramp. "Phil Wilson wants to own the wine and show off how much he paid for it. William Robinson wants to drink it. And I have the distinct impression that Wilson hates to lose."

"That's not exactly news," Paula said. "There was quite a flap a few years back when his sons took over the dealership. It was while you were gone, I think. One of the boys—well, he wasn't a boy, really, he was in his thirties—anyway, he got into drugs and started having financial trouble that threatened the business. Phil came out of retirement and started throwing his weight around.

"He managed to get the son into rehab and the whole thing was hushed up. But I heard there were some nasty arguments out at the cabin while it was going on."

I laughed. "Paula, I can always count on you to know absolutely every story about everybody in town! How do you do it?"

Paula laughed. "Live anywhere long enough and you know where the bodies are buried."

Ahead of me, the empty road disappeared into the darkness outside the range of the headlights. I gave the 'Vette a little more gas, and felt it pull against me, the way the dogs pulled at their leashes. I was already at the limit of safety on the dark, winding road, and it took all my self-control to keep from giving the car its head.

I backed off the throttle as we approached a bend, downshifting before I powered through the curve, then back into fourth as we came out onto the straightaway. This was the part I loved, using the engine and the brakes and the transmission together. When it all meshed, it felt like I was part of the car.

We had dropped the name Veritas, and I was convinced Phil Wilson knew what it was. I still had more questions than answers, but I could feel myself getting closer to a solution. As a bonus, we'd had fun at the auction and now we were flying through the night on our way home.

A perfect end to a perfect evening.

I braked for another curve. The pedal felt a bit mushy. I'd have to get the 'Vette into the shop and have it checked, though I wasn't sure how I'd pay for it right now.

I pushed that worry aside for another day. Tonight I was just enjoying the car. But I did back off the accelerator and let my speed drop.

We passed a "Reduced Speed Ahead" sign, followed by a mileage sign that told us we were two miles from Pine Ridge. I eased up on the throttle.

Almost home.

"Deer!"

Paula's scream came at the same instant my peripheral vision caught a flash of movement at the right side of the road.

I hit the brakes. Hard.

Screeching tires fought to grip the road and I fought to maintain control.

The car slowed.

The deer ran across the highway.

I pulled hard to the right, narrowly missing his powerful kick as he bounded past the headlights.

The brake pedal went to the floor.

And stayed there.

I downshifted, cringing at the roar of the engine as I forced the transmission to absorb the momentum. We slowed, but not enough.

I yanked the wheel to the left, away from the edge of the road, but I overcorrected and drifted across the center line.

I pulled back to the right, stabbing at the brake pedal.

Nothing.

Fighting a growing tide of panic, I reached for the hand brake and yanked as hard as I could.

The brakes locked and the car skidded down the road toward the sign that welcomed us to Pine Ridge.

I struggled to keep the car on the road. I downshifted again and winced at what I might be doing to the engine.

The back wheels broke loose for an instant and the car spun out of control. All I could do was hold on and pray for a soft landing.

The right wheels slipped off the pavement into the gravel on the shoulder. I heard the rattle of stones against the back end.

I could imagine each one ripping into the fiberglass, but I knew the flying stone absorbed energy that would otherwise pour into the wheels. Spinning my wheels in the gravel was preferable to speeding down the highway right now.

As the right wheels spun in the loose gravel the left wheels gripped the asphalt, spinning the car in a one-eighty. Suddenly we were headed back the way we'd come.

The car veered across the highway.

We hit the edge of the pavement, rode up and over a low berm, and nosed into the ditch.

Fiberglass crunched and splintered.

Headlights pointed crazily at the dark night sky, then went out.

The engine died and silence descended.

chapter 24

Paula hadn't spoken since she spotted the deer.

I looked over. Her eyes were wide in terror and her mouth was clamped tight.

"Paula?"

She looked at me, confusion and shock in her expression.

"Paula? Are you okay?"

It took a few seconds for her to unclamp her jaw and answer me. Her voice came out low and shaky, but she was able to speak.

"I—uh—I think so."

I tried to move, but my left hand wouldn't release the steering wheel. I concentrated on unfolding each finger, slowly releasing my grip. It was a slow and painful process.

As I was working to regain the use of my hand, Paula recovered enough to reach her purse and dig in it for her cell phone.

She punched in 9-1-1.

In a few seconds she had a dispatcher on the line. She gave them our location and said we'd had an accident.

"I don't know if there are any injuries." She looked over at me. "Are you hurt?"

"Yeah, I think I am," I said, my voice shaky.

She listened for a moment.

"They're sending an ambulance," she said to me.

In the distance we could already hear sirens approaching. I'd done this twice in the last few days. That was twice too many.

The police arrived first, with fire/rescue and the aid unit close behind.

Soon the car was surrounded by several burly men in turnouts and helmets. After several tries they managed to get the passenger's door open without causing any more damage, which was little consolation given the amount of crackling and crunching I'd heard. Fiberglass cars did not handle impact gracefully.

The car had come to rest with the driver's door pinned against an embankment. I was trapped inside, trying not to think about how much damage that might mean.

"Are you all right?" the paramedic asked.

I fumbled with my seat belt. The latch released and I slid to the right. I was fine until I tried to lean on my left arm to slide over the console.

Pain shot through my wrist and I slipped sideways, unable to support my own weight.

The paramedic was out of his coat and in the passenger's side of the car at once. He put an arm around my shoulders and cradled me against him.

"Stay still," he ordered. "Let me check you over before you try to move."

For several minutes he poked and prodded and carefully manipulated my joints. Except for the left wrist there didn't seem to be any major damage.

The paramedic helped me work my way across the console and out the passenger side of the car.

One look confirmed my worst fears.

The front end of the Corvette was shredded, resin and fabric separated like the layers of a flaky biscuit. The retractable headlights had been ripped from their moorings and dangled by their wires in front of the flattened nose.

My toy was broken. Badly.

I started shaking long before they loaded us into the

ambulance for the ride to the emergency room. A sheriff's deputy wrapped a scratchy blanket around my shoulders, and gave me a chemical hand warmer to hold.

Paula got the same treatment.

I answered a few questions, explaining to the deputy about the deer.

"All this because a deer ran across the road?" He sounded skeptical.

"I didn't want to damage my car," I said. I looked at the wreckage sitting slammed against the embankment. "Not like it helped."

"So you swerved to miss the deer, lost control, and went into off the road? Is that it?"

Another deputy was questioning Paula, keeping her far enough away I couldn't hear his questions or her replies.

"No, that wasn't it. There was a lot more." I tried to explain about sliding and spinning and going back the wrong way.

The deputy looked more and more confused. "Why did you pull the emergency brake?" he asked when I slowed down a little.

"Because the brakes failed." I stopped short. "Didn't I tell you that part?"

From his expression I obviously had not.

I started over with swerving to miss the deer and tried to piece the events together in the correct order. Things were becoming confused in my head, and the pain in my wrist made it hard to think about anything else. It had all happened so fast, and I was shaking so hard my teeth began to chatter.

The deputy signaled the ambulance attendants and we were packed into the back for a ride to the emergency room.

We were met at the emergency entrance by nurses, Sheriff Mitchell, and Sue.

Sue rushed over to me as the nurses helped me out of the ambulance and into a waiting wheelchair. "I'm here if you need me, Georgie," she said, squeezing my hand. The right one, fortunately. "I'll wait until you're through and take you home."

"Dogs?" I croaked. I felt like I couldn't get enough air and my voice wouldn't work right.

"Taken care of," she said.

The sheriff was there in his official capacity, a fact he made abundantly clear by shooing Sue away from me.

"You can talk later."

Sue took the hint and retreated to a seat in the waiting room. She'd brought a book, and as they wheeled us into the treatment room it looked as though she were prepared to wait all night if she had to.

Friends like that are worth more than any car.

Still, every time I thought of the 'Vette stuck against the embankment I wanted to cry. I pushed the thoughts away. Doctors first, mechanics later. And thank God for good insurance on both.

Fred Mitchell followed us into the treatment room and spoke with the attending doctor. "Be sure you get a BAC in addition to whatever else you're doing," he said.

"Don't you need my permission for that, Sheriff?"

"It's routine to ask for it in all accident cases, Miss Neverall. Just figured it was easier to wait until we got you to the hospital." He nodded toward my layers of blankets. "The deputies said you were hurt and they wanted to get you in here as soon as possible.

"And I figured you'd like this a lot better than a field sobriety test," he added drily.

Such a considerate man!

"And if I don't give permission?" I asked.

"We get a court order. Doesn't take long, and we get the same result. Just makes extra work for us and we might need to hold you until we get the order so we can draw more blood." He grinned. "This way is easier for all of us, and then Sue can take you home."

Even in my addled state I noticed that I was once again Miss Neverall, and he had referred to Sue by her first name.

"I haven't had anything to drink, Sheriff Mitchell. Just water. But if it will make you feel better, please take a little extra and satisfy your concerns."

Mitchell didn't rise to the bait. "Thank you, Miss Neverall. Just standard procedure in all accident investigations." He held out a clipboard with a sheet of paper. "Will you sign this release, please?"

I signed and he left.

My indignation stayed. While the doctor examined me I fumed. "What kind of a question is that? Do I want to let him run a blood alcohol test, or do I want to sit in jail while he gets a court order and runs the test anyway? And for what? Because I had a car accident?"

The doctor ignored my ranting and continued with my exam.

He held the stethoscope to my chest and asked me to be quiet and take a deep breath. He made me hold the breath for several extra seconds before allowing me to breathe out.

I took the hint.

The doctor made some notes on his clipboard, then helped me to lay back and stretch out on the exam table. He checked my arms and legs, elbows and knees, taking care not to jostle my wrist, which had swollen alarmingly.

"I don't think we need pictures of anything else," he said at last. "So I'm sending you off to X-ray for that wrist."

The nurse returned and helped me into the wheelchair.

"I'll talk to you when you're through," the doctor said. "For now, just try to relax, if you can."

Easy for him to say. I didn't want to think about how many ways my life was in shambles.

The diagnosis, when it came, was just more of the same.

I'd sprained my wrist. The doctor talked about various grades of injury and said he thought it was only a grade one. I wasn't sure if that was good or bad. Either way, it meant I couldn't work for the rest of the week.

A nurse came in to ask if Mr. Hickey could come back and talk to me.

We'd just been talking about work, and Barry showed

up. It took me a minute to realize why; his wife was in here, too.

"Of course," I said. I turned to the doctor as the nurse hurried away. "That's my boss. *You* can tell him I won't be working the rest of the week."

Barry's reassuring bulk filled the entrance to the treatment cubicle, his broad face troubled. "Are you okay, Georgie?"

"Hey, Bear." I tried to force a note of cheerfulness into my voice, with only modest success. "How's Paula? I haven't seen her since we came in."

"She's okay. A few bruises and scrapes, and she's going to be moving slow for a couple days. But she'll be fine. What about you?"

I pointed to the left wrist the doctor was wrapping in a compression bandage. "Sprained wrist. The doctor says I can't work the rest of the week."

"What kind of work do you do?" the doctor asked, suddenly curious.

"Isn't it on my chart?" I answered. "I thought it would be. I'm a plumber."

The doctor shook his head. "No work this week, and we'll have to see about next. You want to let this heal completely before you put any strain on it." He scribbled a prescription for painkillers and signed it with another scribble.

"You need a ride?" Barry asked as the doctor continued writing.

"Sue's here. She said she'd take me home." I waved my good right hand. "Are they releasing Paula?"

"Said she'd be okay to leave in a couple minutes. If you're sure you don't need anything?" His voice trailed off and he moved a step closer to the door. He was anxious to get Paula out of there.

This was definitely one of those big-brother moments. I grinned at Barry and wished I could hug him. He was one of the good guys and Paula was a lucky woman to have him.

I hoped I would be that lucky someday, but it wasn't something I would admit to my mother.

Mother! Had the sheriff told her about my accident? Could she have heard something, sitting in her cell at the sheriff's station? Would her guards casually mention it, or try to reassure her?

Sheriff Mitchell came back through the doorway. "Can she talk to me now, Doctor?" he asked. When the doctor nodded, he turned back to me. "I need to take an accident report," he said. "Would you rather do this here before they send you home, or at the station on the way home?"

"I'd rather do it tomorrow, when I've had a chance to recover," I shot back. "But I doubt that's an option."

The sheriff quirked one eyebrow. Had Sue told him that was guaranteed to annoy me? "You have a reputation about making official statements," he said. "I'd like to get this done tonight."

I moved my arm to glance at my watch. It wasn't there. All I could see was a mass of compression bandage and a couple shiny fasteners holding the wrapping tight.

I looked up at the clock on the wall. One o'clock.

"You mean this morning," I replied. I might have let it go if he hadn't done the eyebrow thing.

Mitchell gave me a lopsided grin. "All the more reason to get this over with. Sue's still sitting out there waiting to take you home."

I sighed. Might as well get it over with.

"Let me give you the discharge instructions," the doctor said, interrupting our exchange. "Then you can go sit in the lounge. You might be a bit more comfortable there."

Mitchell discreetly withdrew, saying he'd wait for me in the lounge.

I listened carefully to the doctor's instructions, took the pain pills he offered me for tonight since I couldn't fill the prescription until tomorrow, and promised to call my own doctor for a follow-up visit.

"You will not be able to drive for a few days," he advised me. "You have to rest that wrist and allow it to heal."

Outside I nodded in agreement, but internally his advice was filed in the "we'll see" box. After all, I had managed to drive the Beetle with an injured leg, and the automatic stick shift made it possible to drive one-handed.

The sheriff was sitting next to Sue, deep in conversation, when I finally emerged from the treatment room. He stood up at once and motioned to the far corner of the room. I followed him and sat in the chair he indicated.

He could see I was cooperating.

Mitchell pulled out the recorder and I nodded. We'd been through all this before. No need for the preliminaries.

I went through my description of the accident, as I had for the deputy at the scene. This time I was a little calmer and I remembered about the brake pedal the first time through.

"Did you have the car serviced recently?" he asked.

I shook my head. "No," I said for the recorder. "The 'Vette got a full checkup in October, and hasn't been driven much since." I shrugged. "Not a good car for the Great North-wet winters."

The sheriff looked as though he wanted to comment about how well the 'Vette had survived the beginning of summer, but he thought better of it.

"So no one else has had access to the car in several months."

"I keep him garaged, Sheriff. Not the kind of car you leave parked at the curb. But I have driven him a couple times lately. I took him up the mountain a couple days ago, just driving."

"Did you have any problems with the car? Any brake trouble?"

I thought back to my drive on Sunday. I remembered the wind in my hair and the feel of a well-tuned engine responding eagerly to my foot on the throttle. I'd turned around in a rest area just a few miles up the highway, and the car had performed flawlessly.

"Nothing." I shook my head. "He was fine on Sunday." I stopped for a second. "That was just yesterday, wasn't it?" Amazing how time got all twisted around in your head. Sunday felt like several lifetimes ago.

"Yeah." The sheriff looked at the notes he'd taken. "So the car hasn't been out of your control since your previous drive?"

"No. Well, except for the valets."

Sheriff Mitchell was instantly alert. "Of course. You and Ms. Ciccone went to a wine event in Portland, correct? And the car was valet parked?"

"That's correct. We went to an *auction*."

The sheriff colored for a moment. "It's just standard in any accident investigation, Georgie. Makes it easier for everyone involved if there is a question later. If your insurance company raised a stink, for instance, you could point to a clean test." He cleared his throat. "Which, by the way, yours was."

"Told you," I muttered, forgetting about the recorder. My eyes darted to the little machine just as the "Record" light flickered.

Smooth move, Neverall!

The sheriff returned to his questions, asking where and how the car had been parked. I admitted I didn't know where the lot was, just that we had turned it over to the valets in front of Wolfe-Bowers. I remembered thinking it was safer than parking it on the street.

"What's going to happen to my car?" I asked. I wasn't sure I wanted to know. The images in my mind of the shredded front end and crumpled headlights made my stomach hurt and brought tears to my eyes.

"It's being towed," Mitchell said. "They're taking it to the impound yard. One of our mechanics will take a look at it, see if he can determine the cause of the accident. When we're through, you can claim it."

He'd carefully avoided telling me anything about the 'Vette's condition, and I didn't ask. Right now I really didn't want to know.

"I think that's all I need for now," the sheriff said, picking up the recorder and slipping it into the pocket of his shirt. "Do you have any questions?"

I didn't. My wrist throbbed, my head hurt, and all I wanted to do was crawl into a hole and pull it in after me.

The sheriff stood and nodded to Sue, who quickly moved to my side. "Let's get you home," she said. "You've had enough for one day."

She gave the sheriff a look that wasn't meant for me to see. My accident had interrupted their plans, which was why she hadn't gone with me, and now she was leaving him to take me home.

The mention of home finally seeped into my pain-dulled brain. There was something I needed to ask the sheriff.

"Does my mother know about the accident?"

"Why would she?" the sheriff said.

I shrugged, instantly regretting the movement when it wiggled my wrist. "She's in jail, people in the office talk. She might have heard something."

Sheriff Mitchell smiled warmly. "I'll stop by and make sure she knows you're okay," he said. "No sense adding to her worries."

"Thanks," I said. I appreciated his compassion, especially since I had messed up his evening in several ways.

The doctor had given me a sling for my arm and insisted I wear it. It took Sue and Fred together to get me up and into the passenger's seat for the short ride to my house.

chapter 25

By the time we reached my house, the pain pills had started to kick in. The throbbing in my wrist subsided, and exhaustion washed over me.

Sue insisted I get into bed, ignoring my feeble protests that it was my mother's bed for now.

"Well she's not using it and she'll have her own bed back whenever she's able to come home." Sue's matter-of-fact tone left no room for argument. To tell the truth, I wasn't trying very hard. After several days on the couch and an evening on the exam table in the emergency room, the bed looked like heaven.

With Sue's help I got undressed and crawled under the blankets. She fluffed up a pillow and placed it under my wrist, elevating it the way the doctor ordered.

"I'm beat," Sue said. "You ready to sleep?"

I murmured my assent.

"Then I'll see you in the morning." She turned out the light and started to pull the door closed.

"You leaving?" I asked.

"Naw," she answered. "You may need some help in the morning, so I figured I'd stay. Besides," she teased, "somebody has to sleep on the couch."

"Thanks, Sue. I owe you."

The door closed softly behind her.

There was a long list of things to do, but all I wanted was to sleep.

I gave in and closed my eyes.

When I opened them again, the sun was shining through the windows and I could hear Daisy whining at the bedroom door. I knew it was Daisy. Buddha usually waited patiently, but she seemed to lack that ability.

I stretched and was instantly rewarded with pain in my wrist. I froze, then moved carefully to the edge of the bed and sat up. The sudden pain had dissipated, leaving an ache behind to remind me to be careful.

I managed to get into my robe and wobble down the hall to the bathroom by the time Sue caught up to me. "You should have called for help," she said accusingly.

"I can manage." I sounded whiny. "Sorry," I said, more pleasantly. "I think I can shower okay. But I'll holler if I need you. Okay?"

I surprised Sue when I made it to the table without help. She had coffee ready, and I gratefully accepted a cup. "Sorry for interrupting your plans," I said. "I don't think spending the night with *me* was on your agenda."

Sue bristled. "I didn't plan to spend the night with anyone," she said tartly. "You just got lucky."

I rolled my eyes and sipped the coffee before I answered.

"Seriously," I said, "I said I wasn't going to let our friendship screw up whatever you and Fred have going, and I meant it."

"It's really okay. We had dinner and watched a movie, and he was on his way home when the alert came over the radio. He called me as soon as he knew it was your car, said you might need someone. No interrupting."

"Thanks for coming. I really appreciate it."

Sue put a plate of toast on the table and sat down across from me.

"So what are we doing today?"

I thought about the laptop files safely hidden on my thumb drive. "I have some work to do, and you have a business to run."

"Day Spa's closed for the day," she said.

"Sue, this is silly! I have a sprained wrist. I can take care of myself just fine. You go do what you need to." As though to prove my point I picked up a piece of toast with my left hand and took a bite.

She didn't look convinced. "What if you need to go somewhere?"

"I swear I will stay here until you get back." I planned to spend the time trying to unlock the e-mail files.

"You promise?"

"Promise. Scout's honor. I will stay right here."

"Okay." Sue looked relieved. "I have a few deliveries coming this morning. Give me a couple hours. I'll be back before lunch and we can figure out what to do from there."

She gave me an appraising look. "You sure you won't do anything crazy while I'm gone?"

"Go." I waved her away. "I need to do some computer work. No heavy lifting required."

I waited until she was out of the house to fire up the desktop and plug in the thumb drive. Finally I had time to work on Gregory's e-mail files.

First, though, there were a few phone calls I needed to make. I started with the easiest one.

Wade was properly distressed when I told him about the accident, and it took me several minutes to convince him I was fine. Once he accepted my assurances, he wanted to know if there was anything he could do.

"Not unless you know who else was in Veritas," I said, "and I already know you don't. Or if you know what the connection is between William Robinson and Phil Wilson."

"I don't know either one, I'm afraid. And I don't know how they're connected to Gregory." He hesitated, and I heard him draw a deep breath. "I did look back in Gregory's records," he said slowly.

"And?"

"I found a few receipts for Veritas. From the figures he

gave me for his cellaring income, I'm guessing there were four partners. If you're right about Wilson that leaves two more partners out there."

"Which means two people out of the entire population of Pine Ridge." I sighed. "If Wilson is a partner it isn't just year-round people, it could be any of the weekenders, too."

"Everyone except you and Sue and me," he answered. "And William Robinson. He was pretty definite about that."

"Then why was he talking to Wilson?" I was back where I started and it made me crabby. I should be able to figure this out.

On Wade's end I heard his other line ring. It stopped quickly as Karen picked it up, but I knew Wade had work to do.

"I better let you get back to work. I just didn't want you to worry if you heard about the accident." I chuckled. "And in this town I knew you'd hear."

I checked in with Paula. She was stiff and sore, but otherwise undamaged. I assured her I would be fine, and promised to call if I had any news.

The next call was to my insurance agent. While he was dismayed to hear about the 'Vette, he promised to follow up with the impound yard and get some estimates on the repairs.

I didn't tell him I was afraid it was beyond repair. I wasn't ready to admit it, even to myself.

The final call was to the sheriff's office. I spoke to Fred Mitchell and told him the insurance company would be sending someone to look at the car.

"It may be a couple days before I can release it, Georgie. Our accident investigator will be going over it first."

"The brakes failed, Sheriff. Seems pretty simple to me."

"He still wants to take a look."

I asked him about my mother, and he said she was holding up okay. He told me I could visit in the evening if I wanted to come see for myself. I told him I would.

With all the calls out of the way, I settled down with my computer and Gregory's files. I was determined to make use of the enforced down time.

When Sue returned just before noon I had managed to crack the encryption on the files and open the message archive.

But that was only the first step. I was faced with a file full of contacts and incoming and outgoing messages and I had no idea where the information I wanted might be.

If it was there at all.

"This is taking too long," I complained to Sue.

She dropped a white paper bag on the table. "Take a break," she said. "I brought sandwiches from Dee's."

Dee's Lunch was an institution on Pine Ridge's Main Street. Dee had been serving breakfast and lunch—and closing promptly at 2:00 p.m.—for as long as either of us could remember.

One of Dee's sandwiches was reason enough to take a break.

Sue and I ate while I filled her in on the previous night. It was the first time she'd heard the details of the accident, and she was horrified by what happened to the 'Vette. And, like Wade, she couldn't figure out what the connection was between William and Phil Wilson.

Frustration bubbled through me. I couldn't find the information I needed in Gregory's files, I couldn't work, and I couldn't get my mother out of jail.

I needed to do something useful.

And I knew where I had to look.

Mom's backup key ring was on the dresser in the bedroom

On that key ring were *all* her keys.

Including the one to Gregory's house.

◆

Never, ever, ever put coffee grounds or grease down the drain. Most kitchen sink clogs are the result of grease buildup that traps tiny food particles. Better to avoid a clog in the first place than spend time and money clearing it.

—A Plumber's Tip from Georgiana Neverall

chapter 26

Sue was, as usual, underwhelmed with my plan.

"You can't break into Gregory's house. Fred may be sympathetic right now, but if he catches you . . ." Her voice trailed off and her face clouded with worry.

"I won't be breaking in," I argued. "They released the house. I have a key. No breaking in involved."

She looked skeptical. "And what do you hope to accomplish, anyway? The police have already searched the house. If there was anything to find, they would have found it."

"I don't know," I admitted. "But I can't just sit here and do nothing!"

"Yes you can. Remember what happened when you tried to search Martha Tepper's house? Remember how we nearly got caught, and we had to tell Wade what we were doing?"

"This is different."

"How?"

"Wellll . . ." I tried to come up with a good reason, but I couldn't.

"See? It's just the same."

"No, it isn't!" I leaned back and folded my arms.

"Great answer, Georgie," she said sarcastically. "What are you, six? You going to pout?"

"Look, Sue. I have to do something. The police are through with Gregory's house, so what can it hurt for me to go look around? I probably won't find anything," I said before she could start that argument again. "But what if I do? Did the police look for wine records or check out his cellar? Did they even find two hundred cases of wine?"

"Two hundred cases?" She leaned forward, eyes wide. "He had two hundred cases of wine in that house?"

I shrugged. "Wade and I did some checking. I, uh, I managed to retrieve some files from my mom's laptop." I told her about finding the hidden files and breaking the encryption. "We figured there had to be a couple hundred cases owned by Veritas, and Wade said Gregory was storing the Veritas wine.

"So there should be a couple hundred cases of Veritas wine in Gregory's cellar. And who knows how much more of his personal stock?"

Sue gave a low whistle. "So you want to go look for *wine*?"

"And other stuff." I uncrossed my arms and rested my left wrist on the table. It ached and twinged, a constant reminder of my accident.

"I have an idea how to do this without attracting attention."

I laid out my plan, while Sue listened, nodding.

"Okay, Georgie. If I can't talk you out of this, what can I do to help?"

I backed the Rent-a-Dent panel van into Gregory's driveway. I wished we'd had time to get some signs to put on the doors, but the battered, plain white van would have to do.

I'd driven it through a couple mud puddles and artfully splattered more mud over the front license plate. I hoped if any of Gregory's neighbors was watching they would assume it was one of the construction or contractor vehicles that were so common in the neighborhood.

My coveralls strained around my padded torso, disguising the feminine curve of my waist. I'd covered my short hair with a dirty baseball cap and darkened my face with makeup. It wasn't much of a disguise, but I figured I didn't need a lot. People would see the coveralls and tool-box and assume it was a man. That should be enough to make me practically invisible in a neighborhood still un-der construction.

In the back of the van, Sue sat in a folding lawn chair with a book and her cell phone. "I'll call you if anyone comes along," she said. "Be careful, okay?"

I nodded and climbed out of the van. I reached back and took my toolbox in my good hand. I walked up to the front door, selected the key from Mom's key ring, and unlocked the door.

I stepped across the threshold, my heart hammering in my chest, my toolbox a reassuring weight hanging from my right hand, and closed the door behind me.

No turning back now.

I had never been in Gregory's new house before. It had been completed only a few weeks earlier. He and Mom had just started to move in, and it still smelled of fresh paint and new carpet.

The entry was paved with marble tiles set in an intri-cate pattern. The frosted windows surrounding the door soared two stories, flooding the entry with light while maintaining a semblance of privacy.

Ahead of me the entry widened into an airy room with large windows at the far end, overlooking the lush green of the backyard. I remembered Mom talking about the land-scaping project. She and Gregory had planned to be mar-ried there, and Gregory had spent lavishly to create the perfect backdrop for the ceremony that would never take place.

I pushed away thoughts of the wedding.

The dining room was on the right, the kitchen on the left. If I was looking for a wine cellar, the kitchen seemed the logical place to start.

The kitchen was large, packed with every state-of-the-art gadget and gizmo. Custom wood cabinets lined the walls, surrounding the stainless-steel appliances. The counters were a wide expanse of specially ordered granite with two separate sinks and an instant hot water tap.

I checked each cabinet, finding a wealth of top-end small appliances, a pantry stocked with a mixture of staples and gourmet foods, and neatly stacked china and racks of crystal stemware.

No wine.

Several doors led from the kitchen. The first one was a broom closet. No help. The second door opened into a laundry room with a washer, dryer, and several more cupboards and closets. I gave the cabinets a cursory exam, not expecting to find anything. I didn't.

One door left. I turned the knob and pulled but the door resisted. I tugged harder, and it yielded slowly. When it swung wide, I understood why it had been difficult to open. The door opened into a small, refrigerated room, and I'd had to overcome the seal on the refrigerator door.

I'd found Gregory's wine.

I grabbed my phone and called Sue.

The connection was poor, and the signal kept threatening to drop, but I was able to talk to her. "I found the wine," I told her. "Everything okay?"

The connection faded and I stepped back into the kitchen. The signal was stronger. Something in the refrigerated room must be blocking reception.

"Nobody around. Even the neighbors seem to have disappeared." She sighed. "Are you through, then?"

"Give me a few more minutes, okay?"

She sighed again, more dramatically. "Okay, but hurry it up. If anyone checks out this van I am going to look pretty silly sitting here in a lawn chair."

"I'll be out soon," I promised and flipped my phone closed before I went back in the wine room.

Back in the chilly room I took a careful look around. I pulled my notebook from the pocket of my coveralls and started writing notes about what I'd found.

Something wasn't right. It took me a few seconds to figure out what.

The room was chilled. Not just cool, but downright cold. Too cold to cellar fine wine.

And all the wine was white. Not a single bottle of Burgundy or Bordeaux or Pinot Noir.

A rough calculation confirmed what I suspected. There were only about a hundred bottles in the small room. All I had found was the kitchen wine cabinet.

The cellar was somewhere else.

I spent the next twenty minutes prowling through the house opening every door and checking every closet, while fielding increasingly frantic cell calls from Sue.

"Georgie, you have to get out of there."

"What now, Sue?" This was beginning to sound like the boy who cried wolf. "I'd get through a lot faster if you'd stop interrupting me."

That wasn't quite true. I could answer the phone and open closets at the same time. I'd left my toolbox at the door, waiting for my departure. I didn't need to drag twenty-five pounds of wrenches around the house with me.

"One of the neighbors just came home, and he's staring at the van." She sucked in a sharp breath. "He's coming across the street. Hurry!"

"Shoot! Okay, I'll be right there."

I ran for the front door, stuffing my phone and notebook in my pockets. Grabbing the toolbox in my right hand, I twisted the knob and pulled the door open.

Hot needles shot through my wrist and up my arm. Turning the knob with my damaged wrist was a very bad idea.

I bit my cheek to hold back the scream of pain, and fought for control.

Slow even breaths, the way the sensei taught me. Control the breathing, control the body.

My heart still raced, but I presented a calm exterior.

I hoped.

I stepped outside, letting my gaze sweep across the lawn and the street beyond. As Sue had warned, a trim man in a dark suit was walking across the street toward Gregory's house.

I set down the toolbox and pulled the door closed, locking it carefully before turning back around to face the man.

I nearly laughed with relief.

Gregory's neighbor stood at the gang mailboxes on the sidewalk, flipping through a thin stack of envelopes. He looked up and caught sight of me in my coveralls and ball cap. He waved distractedly, and I knew he hadn't taken any real notice of me or the van.

I strolled down the driveway, deliberately taking long strides and rolling my gait slightly as if compensating for the barrel chest and beer belly that strained the zipper of my coveralls. I wanted him to remember a small round man, not a woman.

I tossed the toolbox in the back of the van and opened the top as though retrieving something from inside.

I fought back a giggle when I saw Sue crouched behind the front seat, trying to hide. I stood at the open doors for a minute longer, waiting for the man to move.

He finally glanced back up, saw me fiddling inside the open toolbox, and nodded before walking back across the street. He dropped a handful of junk mail in the trash can next to his garage door and went in the house without another look in our direction.

As soon as he was gone I shut the toolbox, slammed the back doors shut, and climbed behind the wheel. Seconds later we were headed down the street and away from Gregory's house.

Sue didn't say anything until we had put several blocks between us and the house.

chapter 27

"Can I get up now?"

"That might be a good idea," I answered. "Before I get pulled over and your boyfriend, or one of his buddies, gives me a ticket for a passenger without a seat belt."

Sue scrambled between the seats and slid into the passenger's side, hastily dragging the seatbelt across her shoulder and snapping it in place.

My biggest worry right now was where to park the van. I hadn't found what I was looking for so I would have to go back and try again. Parking the van in front of my house in the meantime wasn't a great idea.

"Why don't you put it in your mom's garage?" Sue said. "You have the keys"—she pointed to the key ring hanging out of my pocket—"and Fred's released the house."

The idea appealed to me, but I was reluctant. I hadn't been in that house since the day I'd found Gregory's body, and I wasn't sure I wanted to go back there. It had only been a few days and I wasn't sure I was ready.

On the other hand, it would give me a chance to see the hallway where Gregory had fallen through to the crawl space.

I dropped Sue off at her place to pick up her car. I stopped a few blocks away in the half-empty parking lot of the market. I found a space far enough away from the other vehicles that it afforded a little privacy and did a two-minute makeover, pulling off my coveralls and the padding, wiping my face, taking off my cap, and fluffing my hair with my fingers.

Mom's nosy neighbors would see her daughter in her typical jeans and T-shirt going into the house, not a round man in coveralls.

A few minutes later I pulled the van into Mom's driveway. I left the engine running while I hopped out and used the override key to trigger the garage door opener.

The garage stood empty. Gregory's car had been impounded by the sheriff, and Mom's car was still at the Whitlock Estates office, where she had parked it the day she was arrested.

I parked the van in the garage and closed the door. Running back and forth to operate the door with a key was a nuisance, but it was better than trying to haul the door down one-handed.

The garage was dim and gloomy after the warm sunshine of the early summer afternoon. I shivered and wished I'd brought a jacket. But a jacket wouldn't have taken care of the chill that passed through me.

I debated waiting for Sue. If I had someone with me, it might not be as bad. But would she be willing to help me search the house, or would she dismiss it as a lost cause?

She couldn't argue with me if I was already searching.

I took a deep calming breath, let it out slowly, and unlocked the kitchen door.

The kitchen was as neat as Mom had left it, but there was something just a little off. Things were mostly in the right places, but there were subtle changes. The teakettle that always sat on the left rear burner was on the right rear. The row of canisters—who still used canisters besides my mother?—had the largest one on the left, not the right.

Little things that signaled someone besides my mother had been in the kitchen last. Reminders that the police had searched the house.

I did my best to ignore the evidence of the police search as I prowled through the kitchen. The dishwasher was empty, and I remembered telling Sheriff Mitchell about the dirty glass on the counter.

I riffled through Mom's files in the kitchen, but there wasn't anything I hadn't already seen in the prenup. The one thing I wanted to know about was the one thing Mom was not involved in: Veritas.

I heard Sue's car pull up outside. I walked to the front door and opened it, waving for her to come inside.

While I waited for her to lock the car and come up the walk I glanced up and down the street. Harry Hamilton stood in his living room, watching the street like it was downtown Tombstone and he was Wyatt Earp. Shouldn't he be at work in the middle of Tuesday afternoon?

Sue dragged her feet but eventually she reached the door and came inside. I took a last look at Harry Hamilton and closed the door behind Sue.

I was definitely going to have to do something about Hamilton when I moved in—*if* I moved in. No telling what effect Mom's arrest would have on the sale of the house.

"You got the van put away?" Sue asked.

I nodded. "Locked in the garage. I can take it tomorrow when I go back to Gregory's."

I walked into the living room toward the hallway.

"You said you found the wine," Sue protested as she trailed after me. "What do you need to go back for? You want to sample it?"

"I didn't find it." My voice sounded strange. I was just a couple steps from the hallway, and my throat constricted with dread. I wasn't sure what was in the hall, but I had to see it before I went to see Mom.

The house was cool, but not cold. Still, goose bumps covered my bare arms as I approached the doorway to the hall.

I clamped my jaw tight and stepped through the doorway and into the hall. There wasn't much to see and I exhaled with a rush.

It was a relief, and a letdown.

The rug that normally covered the floor was missing, probably in the same place as the missing dishes. There were two or three dark spots on the wood floor, and the outline of a large square in the middle of the hall.

It was the inside of the hatch I'd seen from under the house. I didn't remember any opening in the floor while I was growing up. It must be a recent modification.

I switched on the light to get a better look at the hatch, and Sue came up behind me. She breathed in sharply when she saw the floor. I followed her gaze and involuntarily made the same noise.

With the light on, it was clear that the spots on the floor were bloodstains.

Gregory's blood.

My ears buzzed and my head felt as though it wanted to drift away from my shoulders and bounce against the ceiling.

It took me a couple minutes of careful breathing and concentration before the light-headed moment passed. Once it did I knelt down, careful to avoid any of the spots. Although they were dry I was loathe to touch them.

I peered closely at the square of flooring that had been cut out of the surrounding floor. The edges had been sanded and sealed, and there was a small recess routed into one side for a finger grip.

I pushed one fingertip into the recess and gave an experimental tug. The hatch moved with surprising ease, and I realized it was hinged on the opposite side. It swung open revealing the empty crawl space.

For a fraction of a second I imagined Gregory's body still beneath the open hatch, the stack of wine crates next to his lifeless form.

Then my eyes focused on the emptiness where his body had been and the image was replaced by one of bare dirt and a square of light shining down through the hole.

I looked carefully at the hatch door. The hinges were designed so that the door could fold back against the floor, allowing unobstructed access to the hole in the floor.

It was a clever design, if you were moving things in and out a lot. Had Gregory been putting enough wine in Mom's crawl space to make that worthwhile? Or had the hatch been built for some other purpose? I couldn't think of a reason, but I would ask Mom when I saw her later.

One more question on the growing list of things I wanted to ask Mom.

I kneeled over and stuck my head in the hole. The crawl space was dark and chilly, with the dank smell of damp soil. There was nothing to see but concrete footings and pier posts disappearing into the gloom.

I sat back on my heels. Sue was right, there was nothing to find in Mom's house. The sheriff would have taken anything significant, yet I suspected very little was missing. They hadn't found anything because there wasn't anything to find.

I pulled the hatch cover back into place with a sigh and stood up.

"Let's go," I said to Sue.

She didn't answer, just turned and led the way to the front door. My disappointment surrounded both of us as we climbed in her SUV for the short drive to my house.

chapter 28

Airedales are a good antidote for a pity party, and mine take their job quite seriously.

As soon as Sue and I opened my door, Daisy and Buddha appeared, begging to go outside. I glanced at Sue and she grabbed the leashes from the hook. A walk would do us all good.

Sue took pity on my injured wrist and handed me Buddha's leash. Today she would take the fractious Daisy.

We made a long, lazy circuit of the neighborhood, walking along the unpaved shoulder of the streets. As though by unspoken agreement we talked about everything except the topic that was foremost in both our minds: Gregory Whitlock's murder.

Sue asked about my upcoming exams. Once I passed the licensing exam I would be a full-fledged plumber. Then what?

It was a good question, and one I had been asking myself.

"Well, since I am buying Mom's house," I said, skipping over all the questions Gregory's murder presented, "I guess it looks like I'm going to stay in Pine Ridge. Barry seems happy with me, and Megan would never forgive him if he lost the only woman plumber on his crew."

"What about Angie? Didn't you say she's started taking the classes?"

The mention of Angie, Barry's receptionist, made me smile. I don't think her ambitions had risen above answering phones and picking up the mail until I went to work for Barry.

Angie had quizzed me several times about the class work, afraid it would be too hard. I had assured her each time that she was capable, and during the slow winter season she had enrolled in her first college class.

"She has a long way to go," I reminded Sue. "It's four years to get a license, at least." I chuckled, remembering Barry's reaction when Angie told him she needed to get off early on Tuesdays for her class. "But I'm betting she'll make it."

"And you?" Sue stopped and turned to look at me. Daisy strained against the leash for a moment, then settled down next to Sue.

I glared down at Daisy. "Traitor!" I looked back at Sue. "You know what happened when I was gone, Sue. My life in high tech stopped being fun a long time before I came running back to Pine Ridge."

I looked around me, admiring the green of the trees. I could hear birds calling in the warm afternoon sun, and the air smelled of freshly cut grass.

"This place isn't perfect," I admitted. "There are things I miss about living in the city. I haven't been to a live theater in three years, unless you count the high school production of *Les Miz*. I haven't had decent sushi, or been able to call out for Chinese. There's no shopping to speak of, and no public transit."

Buddha nuzzled his head against my hand and I scratched his ears.

"But I can walk my dogs, and have time for my friends, and I'm doing work I enjoy. So, yeah. I'm staying here if Barry will keep me on."

Sue laughed. "I don't think there's any question on that

score. He's not about to cross Paula *and* Megan. Not to mention losing his computer guru."

We turned the next corner and headed for home. The dogs strained at their leashes, knowing treats and a nap lay ahead.

"Speaking of computers," Sue said, the caution in her voice warning me that break time was over, "have you found anything in Gregory's e-mail?"

I shook my head. "I got the file open, but I haven't had time to figure out what all is in there. I hope I can figure out some of that tonight."

"I thought you were going to see your Mom tonight."

"I am. But Dave Young's already warned me that I'll probably only be able to stay twenty minutes or so when I visit her, so I should have plenty of time to spend with the computer."

When I unlocked the house the phone was ringing. I tossed Buddha's leash to Sue and ran to the kitchen just in time for the answering machine to click on.

"Georgiana? Dave Young here. Just wanted to verify it's all set for you to visit your mother this evening."

I snatched up the phone. "Dave? So glad you called! How's Mom doing? Is there anything she needs, anything I can take her?" My voice cracked, surprising me. I thought I had adjusted to the fact Mom was in jail.

Apparently not.

"Hi, Georgiana. She's holding up okay. Unhappy, and a little scared, though she isn't likely to admit it." Obviously Dave had caught on to Mom pretty quickly, in spite of her efforts to maintain a stoic façade.

"She's bored, sitting in that cell all day, though. If you could take her something to read, or puzzle books. Something to keep her mind occupied for a few days would be a good idea.

"Anything but murder mysteries." He laughed, but there was nothing humorous in the sound.

"How is the case going?" I asked. "Have you heard anything?"

"Nothing," he answered. "But we're working on it. I expect to get some more information from the prosecutor's office in the next few days, and we'll see what they actually have."

He cleared his throat and continued in a somber tone. "Georgiana, when you visit your mother tonight, please be careful what you talk about. Being in jail means your mother loses a lot of privacy." He paused, then repeated, "A lot of privacy."

I considered his words. "Are you telling me someone might be listening to what we say?"

"The only conversations that are completely protected are the ones with her lawyer, her doctor, and her priest. I'm not saying they will listen in on your conversation. But they can. Okay?"

"Okay. Thanks for the reminder. I'll be careful."

I hung up just as Sue came in the kitchen trailed by two Airedales intent on their post-walk snack. She grabbed a couple green treats from the cupboard and made them both sit before she rewarded them.

I swear my dogs behaved better for her than they did for me.

"Now what?" Sue asked.

I glanced up at the kitchen clock. "Now we eat something before I go see my mother."

"Something" turned out to be canned soup and sandwiches. For all her teasing, Sue wasn't much more of a cook than I was. I wondered aloud if all single women lived on packaged meals and takeout, which earned me a dirty look from Sue.

"I'm just saying, when you're cooking for one, it doesn't seem worth the time and effort to make three-course meals."

Sue put our plates on the table and sat down across from me. "Is that what we've become, Georgie? Those dreaded single women your mother warned us about all those years?"

"Well, we're definitely women, and we're single, so I

guess we fit that definition. But I wouldn't say dreaded." I took a bite of my sandwich. "I don't happen to agree with my mother on that one, as you well know."

"Besides"—I shrugged—"you have Fred. And there's Wade and whatever this thing is we have, which I have decided is definitely a thing, even if I'm not precisely sure where it's going. So we aren't exactly the 'dreaded' single women my mother kept warning us about."

Sue looked amused. "So you're admitting that you and Wade are a thing now? About time!"

I felt a blush climbing my face. "Yeah, I guess I am."

"Even though Mom approves?"

I laughed. "I guess Mom can be right sometimes. It's complicated."

"Everyone's relationships are complicated. Like mine and Fred's. He keeps arresting my friends, or my friends' mothers. And then it's all weird between him and me, and me and my friends, and him and my friends." Sue sighed. "Now, *that's* complicated."

"By 'my friends' I guess you mean me." I chuckled. "I guess I better watch myself or I'll end up sinking your romance."

I thought for a minute. "To be fair, I don't think he actually arrested me. And I get the feeling it was Vernon, the prosecutor, who wanted my mom arrested. I guess Fred didn't have a lot of choice." I shrugged. "It could be worse. At least she's still in Pine Ridge."

"I didn't tell you this, but I know there was an argument with Vernon about that. He wanted to move her to Portland, but Fred wouldn't let him. I'm sure I wasn't supposed to hear it, but it was right there in my kitchen. What was I supposed to do?"

Sue's wide-eyed look of innocence was so fake it made me laugh. "In your kitchen, huh?" I chuckled.

"Okay, Fred's one of the good guys." I sobered. "But I still have to go see my mother, and Dave Young told me to be careful what we say because someone could be listening."

"Yeah, like Douglas Vernon. Be careful."

I nodded and went back to my sandwich.

Forty minutes later we left the dogs napping, and Sue drove me to the sheriff's office. Even though I'd driven the van to Gregory's house, Sue said it would look better if I didn't drive myself to see my mom.

Deputy Carruthers was manning the front desk. He glanced up when we arrived and caught my eye. "Man, Ms. Neverall, I was really bummed to hear about your car. You're gonna need a really good body man. Working with glass is an art. When you're ready, I have a guy up in Sandy who does custom work. I'll have him call you."

His concern for my car was sweet. Carruthers had offered to help me with the Beetle, and had turned out to be a pretty fair shade tree mechanic. I knew I could trust his recommendations.

"Thank you, Deputy. I'll be certain to call you when I'm ready." I smiled, and waited for him to buzz me through the security door.

Once I was inside, Carruthers checked me over with a metal-detector wand like the ones at airport security. He asked for my purse, and told me I could have it back on my way out. He did let me keep the books I'd brought Mom, after he checked those thoroughly, too.

"Procedure," he said with an uncomfortable grimace.

It wasn't like we were fast friends, but we'd formed a bond over my aging Beetle. I liked Carruthers, and I respected his encyclopedic knowledge of early VWs. Going through the security procedure with me was awkward. But it was part of his job.

I was escorted to an interview room to wait for my mother.

Mom had only been in jail a few days, and made a single court appearance, but the strain was evident in her posture and her pinched expression when another deputy brought her in.

She started toward me, like maybe she wanted to give me a hug. Her escort put a hand on her arm, and guided her to a chair, sending a clear signal that there was no physical contact.

We sat opposite each other across a bare, wooden table. The silence stretched. Neither of us knew quite what to say.

"How's your wrist?" Mom asked.

"Just a sprain. The doctor said to take it easy for a couple days and see Dr. Cox for a follow-up."

"Sheriff Mitchell told me you had an accident. I'm glad it wasn't any worse."

With the topic of my accident exhausted we lapsed back into silence. We were both aware, thanks to Dave Young, that we could be overheard. It put a definite crimp in the conversation.

"I brought you some books." I set the stack of paperbacks on the table. "I wasn't sure what you'd want, so I tried to get a few different things. Just let me know if you want something in particular."

"Thank you."

Silence.

This was getting increasingly uncomfortable. I wanted to see Mom, to see for myself that she was okay, but I didn't know what to say to her. There were things I wanted to ask, but I couldn't. Not when Vernon could be listening.

I decided there was one thing I could ask, something that didn't really have anything to do with Gregory. I hoped.

"Mom? There is one thing I don't understand. Where did that hatch in the hallway come from? I don't remember it being there when I lived in the house."

"Oh, that." She seemed relieved to have something to talk about. "About the time you went off to that school, your father thought he was going to put in an air conditioner. For some reason he decided it should go under the house." She shook her head at the memory. "He was a lot of things, but practical wasn't one of them."

There was a hint of affection in her voice, something I

hadn't heard from her in a long time. Maybe she was finally moving past the bitterness and resentment. Maybe.

"Anyway, he had that hole cut in the floor, so that he could bring in this whatever-it-was that wouldn't fit through the outside access hole.

"Then he wanted to get it hooked into the heating ducts so it would cool the whole house. That's when he found out it would never work."

"He wanted to put the thing *under* the house?"

"I know," she replied. "Besides that, he found out that the piece he cut out would fall through into the crawl space and he had to go down there and haul it back up. That was when he hired a carpenter to come and put hinges on it."

Mom shook her head. "I just covered it up with a rug and I'd really forgotten all about it until—" She stopped suddenly, refusing to take the thought any further.

"This is ridiculous!" she burst out. "Do you *know* what they said, Georgie?"

I stared, not knowing what to say.

"They said he was stabbed, with a knife from my kitchen! My knife! That horrible man"—I assumed she meant Vernon—"said there was a knife missing and that I must have thrown it away somewhere after I stabbed him."

She leaned forward, bracing her arms against the edge of the table. "Those were my Global knives, Georgie. I wouldn't *do* that to my knives!"

I remembered the knives in her kitchen, carefully arrayed in the stainless-steel block on the countertop. I couldn't remember seeing the block when I was in the house, another of the clues the house had been searched.

"I know that, Mom," I said in what I hoped was a soothing tone. "I know you didn't do this. It's impossible."

There, the one topic we'd been avoiding was out in the open. We were talking about it, and the world didn't end.

We could get through this.

There were questions I wouldn't ask, however. I didn't

dare tip my hand to Vernon. He was intent on convicting my mother and I was intent on getting her released.

I kept my plans to myself.

We retreated to careful conversation about the weather and the dogs and when I could go back to work, and my twenty minutes flew by. Before I knew it, Carruthers was in the doorway, signaling that the visit was over.

"You can come back tomorrow after she has dinner," he said as he escorted me down the hall toward the front door.

He paused a few feet from the door to the lobby. He glanced around as though checking he wouldn't be overheard, and spoke softly. "She'll be okay, Ms. Neverall. She's strong.

"Same time tomorrow," he said in a flat tone as he opened the door and returned my purse. "Please call if you will be delayed."

I walked through the door and back into the normal world, the world where people were free to come and go as they pleased, and to reach out for a hug when they needed one.

Which is precisely what Wade offered.

I stood close to him and let him wrap his arms around me. The warmth of his chest against my cheek was pure comfort, and I soaked it in.

Wade kept his arm around my shoulders as he guided me toward the door and out to his car.

"I thought Sue was going to wait for me," I said, finally realizing the switch in escorts.

"I called her, told her it was my turn to take care of you for a while." He shrugged. "I figured maybe you could use a beer, or something stronger. How about Tiny's?"

I shook my head. "I have stuff to do at home, Wade. But I have a couple microbrews in the refrigerator. Change in plans?"

"Sure."

We were back at my place before I was able to talk

about what I had seen. "She was all over the place. Quiet and subdued one minute, ranting and raving the next, and then quiet again.

"I know she's stressed out, but she wasn't the Mom I was used to. I felt bad for her, but I have to admit, it creeped me out."

"We'll get her through this," Wade promised. "She's got a lot of people on her side. You, me, Sue, Dave Young. We're a good team."

The mention of Mom's lawyer reminded me of something. "Can you get hold of Dave?" I asked. "There were a couple things I wanted to ask Mom, but I didn't want to ask her myself." I repeated Dave's warning about privacy.

"I'll have him call you." Wade hesitated. "What's this about, Georgie? Is there any way I can help?"

I took a deep breath and plunged in. "What do you know about Gregory's house? The one he had built?" I hurried on, trying not to think about the risk I took by telling him what I'd done.

"I was out there," I said. "This afternoon." I held up a hand. "I know what you're going to say. Don't. I had Mom's key and the house is hers, so I had every right to be there.

"I didn't find the wine, Wade. There should have been two hundred cases of wine, Burgundy and Bordeaux and Syrah, and there wasn't a single bottle of red wine in the house. All I found was a refrigerated cabinet the size of a closet with some whites and a few sparkling wines.

"No red."

"There has to be," Wade said. His brow furrowed with worry. "There has to be or Gregory was involved in a scam of immense proportions. He had an insurance rider put on the place for a quarter million on wine, and he was getting storage fees from Veritas for the bottles that were on that spreadsheet you found.

"It has to be there."

We went back and forth about what it meant that I

hadn't found the wine. Wade was adamant that it was there and I had missed it. He couldn't believe that Gregory had lied.

We hadn't settled anything by the time he left, and I didn't tell him I was going back to have another look.

I think he knew anyway.

chapter 29

After Wade left I settled down with a cup of tea and the computer files. It was late, but I didn't have to get up for work in the morning. The search for Gregory's files was pulling me back into the world of all-night computer sessions.

It was familiar territory.

Picking apart the e-mail archive was tedious. My tea grew cold and my neck stiffened. It was more of a challenge with one hand, but I meticulously followed each thread and link, re-creating the original files.

It was like untangling a knotted ball of yarn, and it required patience and discipline. Pull one thread the wrong way and it tightened into an unyielding mass.

The reward for my patience came in the wee hours of the morning. I found the encryption key for the address file, and all at once I had Gregory's contacts.

Names, companies, e-mail addresses—some even had phone numbers. There were address groups, too. Including a group named Veritas.

I'd found Gregory's partners.

Excitement shot through me, a bolt of energy like the rush from a triple-shot mocha with extra chocolate syrup.

I tracked the names in the group to the individual e-mail addresses within the contacts file. Phil@WilsonAutoGroup.com was obvious, as was GWhitlock@WhitlockEstates.com.

The other two were a little more difficult.

I started backtracking the names through domain registries, and found Taylor Parkson behind another one of the addresses. No surprise.

The fourth address was my downfall. The domain, wineconsultantsoregon.net, ended in a proxy site. Proxy sites provided an anonymous registry for domain names, and they prided themselves on their ability to disguise the identity of the actual registrants. Even with my skills I couldn't crack the wall surrounding the site's records. And without a warrant they weren't going to share any information with me.

For once, a computer problem stopped me in my tracks.

I stretched, feeling the muscles in my neck and back creak in protest. My right hand was cramped and aching from doing the work of both hands. I yawned so wide I thought my jaw might never close again.

Time to sleep.

Dogs do not have any respect for all-nighters. No matter how late I went to bed, they expected me to get up and let them out as soon as the first rays of morning sun reached the backyard. They also have the uncanny ability to force you to wake up by staring at you.

Which is what Daisy did way too early the next morning.

While the dogs explored the backyard—in case it had changed overnight—I called Dave Young. Although it was early, he was already at his desk, and sounded as though he had been up for several hours.

I told him about my visit to the sheriff's station the night before and the invitation to return.

"It's good for her to be able to see you," he said. "But it must be hard for you."

"I'm okay for now," I told him. I wasn't sure it was true, but I had to do what I could.

And one of the things I could do was look for the missing wine.

I asked Dave if he could talk to Mom about Gregory's wine cellar. I didn't explain why, and although it must have sounded like an odd request he didn't ask. I had the feeling he didn't want to know. Besides, if I was wrong, if somehow there wasn't any wine, then I'd look like an idiot.

I hate looking like an idiot.

Better to wait until I had something useful to tell him.

I went back to work on Gregory's files, and halfway through my second pot of coffee I struck more pay dirt.

This time it was actual mail archives. The message files had been zipped and encrypted, but I teased out a string of messages and slowly unraveled the entire file.

Now I had the actual messages that went with the addresses, and it was fascinating reading. One message header in particular caught my eye: "Authentication Report, Lot 755."

I scrolled down to the mail and began to read with a growing sense of dread. Gregory had hired a wine expert to check on a lot he'd bought in an online auction.

A lot that had been shipped from Paris—France, not Texas.

There were four cases in the lot, and he had paid five figures a case. The total outlay was nearly fifty grand.

The expert's opinion was that the wine was counterfeit.

Worth about fifty bucks a bottle.

That was bad news when he'd paid almost a thousand bucks a bottle. It was also several thousand reasons to kill him.

But there were several big ifs between the e-mail in the file and Gregory's body under Mom's house, and I had no way to prove it was connected.

I wasn't sure who I could trust with the information I'd found. Dave Young was the likeliest candidate, but when I tried to reach him he was out of the office.

In a perfect world I would turn the information over to the sheriff and he would be able to find the connections that would lead him to the killer.

But in a perfect world he wouldn't have arrested my mother in the first place.

I tried to keep busy around the house, waiting for Dave Young to call me back. I told myself there wasn't anything I could do until I knew if the wine was in the house.

But something in the back of my brain kept nagging at me. There had been something odd about Gregory's house, something that didn't fit. And I had to know what it was.

This time I went alone.

I drove the Beetle to Mom's house, thankful for the automatic stick shift, and switched to the rented van. I changed into my coveralls and padding, and put on my ball cap. I was ready to explore Gregory's house again.

This time I put a grid pad and several pencils in the top tray of my toolbox. There was something wrong with my mental picture of the house. There should be a wine cellar, a large one, somewhere in that building and I was determined to find it. If that meant drawing out every square foot of the house, that was what I would do.

I forced myself not to look at the house across the street as I backed the van into the driveway. I didn't know if the guy was home, but if he was I didn't want him to notice me noticing him. A workman arriving to finish a job would pay no attention to the neighbors.

I locked the front door behind me and left my toolbox in the entry. I would retrieve it on the way out. Taking my cell phone, the grid pad, and a couple pencils, I set out to study Gregory's house.

There was a secret here, and I had to find it if I wanted to get my mother out of jail.

And no matter how crazy she made me, I wanted my mom to be a free woman again.

I started with the entry, estimating the size of the room and making note of doors and windows. I had a measuring tape in my toolbox, but I was already juggling paper and pencil and the tape would have been impossible one-handed.

I could come back with Sue later, if I had to, but I didn't want to get her in any deeper than she already was. I would manage alone for now.

The sun crept across the great room as I worked my way through the house. A map of the house began to emerge, taking shape in smudged pencil lines and erasures, in squiggles and arrows and scribbled notes.

At last there was one large blank area left. The place I knew I would eventually have to go. The one place I wasn't sure I could face.

The master bedroom.

Somehow, invading the private room my mother had shared with Gregory would cross a barrier in our relationship, even if she never knew I'd been there.

I would know I'd been there. I'd invaded her privacy. Whatever I saw couldn't be unseen. It would be in my brain forever.

What was I, nine? It's just a bedroom. Get over yourself, Neverall.

I squared my shoulders, took a deep breath, and opened the door.

The room looked like something in a magazine layout. Every detail was perfect. Unlike my house, there were no dirty socks on the floor, or books left splayed open across the night table. No jumble of pocket debris on the dresser, or empty water bottles next to the bed.

This was what I was obsessing about? I'd driven myself crazy avoiding *this*—a room that looked like no one lived there?

I laughed at myself, and the sound echoed through the empty house. It was a sudden reminder that I was alone in a strange house that belonged to a dead man.

A shiver ran down my spine, and it felt as though someone was watching me.

It was silly—all the doors and windows were locked—

but I still found myself looking over my shoulder, wondering if I could have somehow left something open.

I knew I hadn't, but the feeling persisted until I gave in to my growing paranoia. I backtracked to the entry and double-checked the front door. It was securely bolted.

I hadn't opened any windows or any other door. It was nothing more than an overactive imagination and maybe a guilty conscience.

I went back to work.

When I got to Mom's closet I gasped aloud. I'd swear it was as big as my bedroom, maybe bigger. Big enough to hold a dressing table and a jewelry armoire as well as custom-fitted rods and shelves, and an array of sweater boxes and shoe racks.

Especially shoe racks. There must have been at least thirty pairs of stiletto heels in a rainbow of colors and styles. The one thing they had in common was the high, thin heel that had become Mom's trademark.

I didn't see a single pair of flat shoes in the entire closet.

Gregory's closet, in contrast, was fairly modest. It held several racks of suits and sport coats, and stacks of carefully starched and pressed dress shirts.

But it looked tiny next to the luxurious indulgence of what could more properly be called my mother's dressing room.

I was sketching in the bedroom wing when my cell phone rang. The sudden noise in the empty house set my heart racing.

I dropped the pencil and fumbled for the phone with one hand. The number wasn't one I recognized.

"Hello?" I answered in a voice just above a whisper. Somehow I couldn't bring myself to speak out loud.

"Georgiana? Dave Young here."

I breathed a sigh of relief and replied in a slightly more normal tone. "Hi, Dave. Have you seen Mom?"

"I just left her," Dave replied. "She's doing okay.

"The reason I called," he continued, "is that I asked her

about the wine cellar. She thought it was a pretty random question, but she did say he had a large storage cellar."

"Did she say where the cellar was, Dave?"

"Just that he'd had it specially built into the new house."

There was a minute of silence on the other end of the line. I could imagine Dave trying to figure out why I had asked. But he still didn't question me.

There didn't seem to be anything left to say. I thanked Dave for calling and hung up.

I had confirmation there was a storage cellar, but not where it was.

I went back to my sketches.

chapter 30

Something was wrong with the proportions in my drawing. I twisted the page around, looking at it from different angles, trying to figure out where I messed up.

It wasn't something wrong, it was something *missing*.

Just like the files on Mom's laptop, there was a space with nothing in it.

It had to be the wine cellar.

I paced off the bedroom. The closet doors were on one long, windowless wall. But when I compared the inside of the closets they didn't add up to the length of the wall.

I paced the wall again. Mom's closet. Gregory's closet. And a wide expanse of wall with no door.

What was on the other side of that wall?

I went back into Gregory's closet, and flipped on the light to look at the wall next to the missing space. A rod spanned about half the wall, suits and sport coats carefully spaced along it to prevent wrinkling. Gregory was always impeccably dressed.

Below the rod was a chest with partitions sized to hold shoes. Several of the spaces were empty, as though Gregory didn't have enough shoes to fill the chest.

But when I bent over to look more closely, I realized the empty spaces had recessed handles inside them. They were meant as handholds to move the chest.

I held my breath and reached for the right side handle. As soon as I gripped it, I felt a latch release, but the chest wouldn't budge.

I tried releasing each side, but the minute I let go of a latch it snapped closed again. In order to move the chest I had to trip both latches at the same time.

I tried to use my left hand to hold the latch, but the pain in my wrist was too great and I lost my grip.

I bit down on my bottom lip and forced myself to try again. I ignored the pain, refusing to surrender to it. The fact that there were hidden latches meant there was something important to hide, and I had to find it.

I drew in a deep breath and braced for another wave of pain as I curled my fingers around the latches and pulled.

I nearly toppled over backward when the latches released and the chest slid easily away from the wall, revealing the bottom of a door.

The upper portion of the door was still covered by the wall behind the clothes rod. It took me a few more minutes to find the release, but then the entire section of the closet swung away, exposing a simple door with a deadbolt.

I took Mom's keys out of my pocket and tried the front door key. To my surprise, it worked. All the locks in the house were keyed alike, even the hidden one.

Chalk one up for the efficiency of master keys.

I'd found Gregory's wine cellar.

The room was a couple steps down from the rest of the house. I suspected it sat on a slab to take advantage of the natural cooling, rather than on a foundation like the rest of the house.

It was a big room, chilly but not cold. Wooden racks lined the walls on three sides. The fourth wall, where the door was, held a counter with several notebooks, each spine labeled with a variety of wine.

I picked up a book at random and flipped quickly through the pages. They were inventory books, listing the wine, its purchase date, cost, and cellar location.

Looking from the book to the racks, I was able to figure out the location key. Each rack had an alphabetical designation and the rows were numbered from top to bottom and left to right.

If I wanted the bottle listed at the top of the third page, it was in rack C, row five, bottle two.

To test my theory I carried the book over to rack C and compared the label with the entry. It was a match.

I could have spent several hours checking the contents of the cellar against the listing, but I didn't want to leave the van parked in the driveway. I'd already been there longer than I wanted to be.

I did a quick count of the racks and bottles before I closed the door and returned the clothes rod and chest to their places.

I scribbled the estimate on the corner of my sketches and headed for the door. Time to get out.

I drove away from Gregory's with a growing sense of excitement. I'd found the wine and I had the names of Gregory's partners.

Now all I had to do was figure out how to use that information to get my mother out of jail.

Minor detail.

Back home after switching vehicles at Mom's, I let the dogs out and considered my next move. The day's activities had left my wrist throbbing and my stomach in knots.

I sat down with the computer to compare my notes with the information I already had, and found a discrepancy. The rough count I'd done in the wine cellar was several cases short of the totals shown on the spreadsheet.

Were those the cases that had been found with Gregory's body? And were they the same cases that were listed in the Authentication Report?

And if they were, how did four cases of counterfeit wine end up under my mother's house? With the dead body of her fiancé?

The situation was getting stranger by the minute.

I needed options, and I wasn't seeing very many. I'd already decided against going to the sheriff. He would have to turn everything over to Vernon, a man I did not trust. I wasn't sure how Dave Young would react to my search of Gregory's house.

He might even have to tell the Deputy Prosecutor, and given Vernon's pursuit of my mother I didn't doubt he'd be happy to put me in an adjoining cell, even if he had to settle for a trespassing charge until he could think of something worse.

My brain was stuck in a rut, and I couldn't seem to find my way out. I needed to make something happen, and I had a way to do just that.

I opened my e-mail program and copied the names and addresses from Gregory's Veritas list. I had Phil Wilson, Taylor Parkson, and the mysterious wineconsultantsoregon.net.

If I e-mailed the three partners, maybe I could stir up some action. And maybe I could find the face hidden behind the anonymous address.

I wrote and rewrote the e-mail, trying to get the proper tone. I debated about a salutation, but couldn't come up with anything I liked so I simply started with the message, told them I had the wine, and asked what they wanted to do with the hundreds of bottles that would soon be homeless.

It was an exaggeration, of course.

Gregory had changed his will several months earlier, when he started building his new house. Mom was his sole heir and when she got out of jail she would decide whether to continue storing the wine in Gregory's cellar. In the meantime it was safe in the house as long as the climate-control system was active.

But it was the easiest way to get their attention.

I wasn't sure what I would do when I heard from them, but it was a first step. And I still had the Authentication Report, which I hadn't mentioned. I was saving that for later.

I had learned the hard way about facing off with suspects on my own. If I was going to meet with the Veritas partners, I didn't want to go alone.

I knew I was pushing the limits of my own "go slow" edict. I weighed the potential risks involved. And then I called Wade.

I told him I had found Gregory's wine cellar, and that there were a couple thousand bottles in the hidden room behind Gregory's closet. I even described the location of the room.

Wade gave a low whistle. "Pretty fancy detective work, Georgie. Ever thought of joining the sheriff's office?"

I wasn't sure he was entirely joking. We'd had several discussions about the all-male force in Pine Ridge. From Wade's seat on the City Council he'd had an inside look at the difficulties of recruiting a female deputy into a rookie position on a small-town force with few opportunities for advancement.

"I'd end up riding a desk and running a computer all day," I answered. "No thanks."

I went back to my original question. "Wade, I may have to go talk to these guys and I don't want to go alone." I swallowed hard. Asking for help was always difficult for me, and this time there were some relationship implications I didn't want to think about too hard. "Will you go with me?"

There was silence at the other end of the phone connection, and I babbled on. "I know this is asking a lot. Even if I have the keys to the house, and even if it technically is my mother's now because she's Gregory's heir, I know you don't approve.

"But proving I know where the wine is might be the only way I can convince these guys to talk to me, and that's the only way I can find out who killed Gregory—"

"Yes." Wade's single word answer stopped my dithering.

"Yes, you don't approve? Or, yes, you'll go with me?" I held my breath and waited for his answer.

"Yes, I'll go with you." There was a deep sigh on Wade's

end of the conversation. "I have learned that there's no way to stop you once you've decided to do something, and it's clear you have, haven't you?"

"Yeah."

"So, with or without me, you're going, aren't you?"

"Yeah," I said softly. "I guess I am."

"Then I can't very well say no. It would just mean you'd go alone, and I think you could use some backup.

"So call me if you have to go out there, okay?"

I agreed, and Wade changed the subject. "How is your wrist? Is it healing at all?"

"Still hurts, but I think it's getting better. I have an appointment in a couple days to have Dr. Cox check it."

"How about the car? Have you heard anything?"

"Not yet. The insurance company is supposed to be sending an adjustor to assess the damage, but I don't know if they've been out yet or not.

"You're the one who knows everybody in town, Wade. What have you heard?"

"Nothing much," he admitted. "But Louie Marks was making a lot of noise at Tiny's about how he kept that car in perfect condition, and there's no way it should have lost control like that, unless you were driving crazy."

"I wasn't!" I protested. "I was driving the way I usually do. Which, I admit, is a little fast. But nothing crazy."

I remembered the sickening feeling as the brake pedal dropped to the floorboard. "I'm sure the brakes failed, Wade. One minute everything was fine and seconds later I was out of control and the brakes didn't work."

"Maybe the sheriff will find some explanation, or the insurance adjustor will." He paused. "I probably shouldn't have told you what Louie said. I'm sorry."

"Don't be. He's right. I had the car in there regularly, and he kept everything running right. We both took good care of the 'Vette, and he's probably feeling almost as bad about it as I am."

I shook off the melancholy that threatened to descend. I wasn't ready to think about the 'Vette. As long as the sheriff and the insurance adjustor were continuing their investigations, I could delay making any decision.

I was good with that.

I reminded Wade he'd offered to drive me over to see Mom after work. He promised to pick me up, and offered to swing by Garibaldi's while I talked to my mother.

Wade was definitely working his way into keeper territory.

Flush your drain-waste and vent systems regularly. Each time you get up on the roof to clean your downspouts and gutters, run a garden hose into each vent. A couple minutes of water at full flow should do the trick. If you're not fond of going on the roof yourself, ask the people you hire to clean your downspouts and gutters (and you should do that at the end of every autumn) to do it for you.

—A Plumber's Tip from Georgiana Neverall

chapter 31

My visit with Mom was as awkward as it had been the night before. She asked how I was, I told her I was getting better. She said she was innocent, and railed against the sheriff and the prosecutor.

When Carruthers knocked on the door and told us our time was up, I was relieved. Mom might need to see me, to be reminded she wasn't alone, but seeing her in such distress took a toll.

As I walked through the door into the lobby I felt as though a huge weight had been lifted from my shoulders. Even as a visitor, being behind the locked security doors and under the watchful eyes of the ever-present deputies felt oppressive.

Wade waited in the lobby, as he had the previous night, and we hurried out the door to his car. I slid into the passenger's seat and Wade handed me the pizza box from the backseat. The aroma of tomato sauce and pepperoni filled the small car and made my mouth water.

"Extra onion?" I asked hopefully.

Wade grinned. "As long as we're both eating them it's okay, isn't it?" He closed the car door and moved to the driver's side.

As he slid in, I leaned over and kissed his cheek. "In case the onions prove too much," I teased.

He turned and gave me a real kiss, then started the car. "If it's just in case, better make it worthwhile," he said.

The dogs were waiting when we got home, but they had to settle for a romp in the yard and a green treat instead of the pepperoni and cheese they felt they deserved. Daisy's reproachful look said more clearly than words that I was a mean and neglectful Airedale mom.

While we ate I filled Wade in on all the information I had been able to glean from Gregory's e-mail archive. He raised his eyebrows when I told him about the report indicating some of the wine was counterfeit.

"You mean it's worth about ten cents on the dollar? That's going to be a pretty big hit for his partners."

"Big enough to get him killed?" I asked. "I mean, sure it's a lot of money, but do you think somebody would actually kill him over it?"

Wade shook his head. "Who knows? But if you think somebody killed Gregory because they lost money on this wine deal, shouldn't you be talking to the sheriff about it? He's the one who should be chasing these guys, not you."

"Can you just hear that conversation? Sheriff Mitchell I have some information that might bear on your investigation. How did I get this information? Oh, I just happened to hack into my mother's laptop and find some of Gregory's hidden files. Why, no, I didn't think I should tell you about them. Withholding evidence? Hindering an investigation? But I'm here *now*." I shook my head. "I don't think I want to go there."

"And how is what you're doing any better?"

This was like talking to Sue. I didn't have a good answer for Wade, either. "Because," I said lamely, "maybe if I can solve this for him, he won't think about arresting me."

We talked as we finished the pizza. Wade couldn't change my mind about going to the sheriff. I think he knew he wouldn't but hc had to try.

After dinner I showed Wade the report from the wine expert, and the comparison between the spreadsheet and the rough count I'd made in the wine room. I could see it was making an impression on Wade.

I kept refreshing my e-mail every few minutes, hoping I would hear from at least one of the Veritas partners. Not that I was sure what I would do when I did, but I couldn't resist checking again and again.

Wade left early, after extracting a promise from me not to go anywhere without him. It didn't matter, though, since I hadn't heard from any of the Veritas partners. Maybe I had overestimated their concern.

Or maybe none of them was involved.

The ringing phone raised my hopes. Maybe one of the partners had decided to call me instead of answering my e-mail.

But when I answered it was Fred Mitchell's voice on the other end of the line.

"What is it, Sheriff? Is something wrong with Mom?" I had just been there a couple hours earlier, but I could imagine dozens of dramatic scenarios with my mother center stage.

"She's fine, Georgie. I was actually calling about your accident. I was still here when the accident investigator came in with his report. I thought you needed to know what he found."

There was that tone of voice again, the one that told me he was going to say something I didn't want to hear. I'd been hearing that tone far too often lately.

"What he found?" What did that mean?

"He completed his examination of the car this afternoon and just finished writing up his report. I don't want to add to your worries, Georgie, but it appears that the brake lines were damaged before the accident. He couldn't say for certain, but he believes they were cut."

I froze. My brain refused to process his words, to accept the implication that someone meant to hurt me.

"Georgiana? Are you still there?" I'd been silent long enough to worry the sheriff.

"I'm here, Sheriff. But that can't be right."

"My expert thinks it is. And I trust his opinions. I don't mean to alarm you, but I want you to be cautious—and I know that isn't your usual mode. Will you just be careful, and let *me* take care of finding out what happened here, please?"

I gave the sheriff my word that I wouldn't interfere in his investigation. Besides, as far as I could tell he was only talking about the investigation of the accident.

I didn't make any promises about Gregory's murder.

After the sheriff's call, I couldn't relax in my own house. I jumped at every noise, and found myself prowling from one room to the next as though I expected to find someone hiding behind the couch, or in the linen closet.

Had I made myself a target? And was someone lurking in the dark, ready to attack?

This was ridiculous! I told myself I didn't believe anyone had done anything to my 'Vette. The brakes failed. Things happened when a car was old. That was all.

I checked my e-mail one more time, then checked the locks and went to bed.

The dogs were barking. Even Buddha, normally calm and patient, demanded I get up.

I tossed back the covers and shushed them. Whatever doggy emergency they felt demanded my presence could wait until I pulled a bathrobe around me.

I shuffled to the back door, Daisy and Buddha dancing around my feet. I figured I should be grateful they woke me up instead of ruining the carpet, but gratitude wasn't in my vocabulary first thing in the morning.

I opened the back door and they shot through into the backyard. The *dark* backyard.

I peered at the kitchen clock. They needed to chase a cat out of their yard at three in the morning?

I stood at the door and called softly for the dogs. Buddha returned immediately, but Daisy took another minute to assure herself the yard was safe from intruders.

Intruders? I remembered Sheriff Mitchell's phone call. What if the intruder was something a little bigger than a cat?

I called Daisy again, urgency making my voice tremble.

To my amazement, she appeared at once.

I slammed the door behind her and flipped the deadbolt.

I told myself it had to be a cat. Or a squirrel. Or even another dog. That was all. I was letting the sheriff's warning make me paranoid.

So why couldn't I get back to sleep?

I spent the rest of the night huddled on the sofa, wrapped in an old quilt like a child with a security blanket and watching increasingly bad movies. I didn't nod off again until the sun streaked the early morning sky with pink, and the cheery voices of the local morning newscast replaced the movies.

A few hours later I woke up again to sunlight streaming between the curtains and the dogs snoozing contentedly in their beds, the excitement of the pre-dawn hours forgotten.

I couldn't forget it quite so easily. I was stiff and sore, and my wrist ached from being cramped against my chest, clutching the quilt.

I stretched and yawned. Three hours of fitful sleep sitting on the sofa was no substitute for a night's sleep in my own bed.

I shambled to the bedroom dragging the quilt with me. I dropped it in a heap on the unmade bed and glanced at the clock.

Ten fifteen.

I had an appointment with Dr. Cox in half an hour.

Fortunately, everything in Pine Ridge proper is five minutes from everything else. That includes my house and the doctor's office. I even had time for a quick shower and a change of clothes before I pulled the Beetle out of the driveway and onto the road.

Three blocks from the house, I approached the first stop

sign. I reached for the brake pedal and felt panic flood through me. The Beetle had been in the driveway all night, unprotected.

What if the sheriff was right, and someone had deliberately cut the brake lines on the 'Vette? They could have done the same thing to the Beetle.

I gingerly touched the brake pedal, holding my breath and tensing in anticipation of the sickening slide that I'd felt in the 'Vette.

The brakes grabbed gently and the car slowed. I released my breath and pressed the brake pedal, bringing the car to a stop at the intersection.

I drove the rest of the way to the doctor's office feeling foolish and melodramatic.

The visit with Dr. Cox was uneventful, as was the trip home afterward. He informed me that my wrist was healing but I would be off work a few more days. He rewrapped the bandage and repeated the instructions I'd been given in the emergency room.

I let the dogs out when I got home and followed them into the backyard. As far as I could see there was nothing to account for their early-morning meltdown. No broken bushes or trampled flowers. Nothing to indicate it had been anything other than what I suspected—a neighborhood cat or a stray dog.

Nothing to get excited about outside.

Back inside I did find something to get excited about.

An e-mail from wineexpert@wineconsultantsoregon.net.

chapter 32

I clicked on the e-mail with trembling fingers. I had my first direct communication from one of the Veritas group; from the one partner I didn't know.

"Thank you for your message regarding the inventory owned by Veritas Partnership. As an investor in Veritas, I am, of course, concerned that the assets be held in optimum conditions. Please advise us regarding the time frame you anticipate for relocating the inventory, and the current location of said inventory."

He'd sent copies to the other partners, but I wasn't sure whether he was speaking for the group or just assuming the role of spokesman.

I sent a cautiously worded reply, assuring all the partners that the wine was stored appropriately. I didn't offer an answer to his question about time.

A few minutes later I had an e-mail from Phil Wilson. I noticed he didn't bother to include his partners in his response. All he wanted to know was whether all the bottles were intact. His tone made it clear his only concern was his investment.

I replied that none of the wine in the cellar appeared to be disturbed.

I deliberately neglected to mention the missing bottles. If he suspected there were bottles missing, he hadn't said so, and I wasn't going to volunteer any information.

I got up to make a sandwich and a cup of coffee. By the time I came back to the computer, I'd heard from Taylor Parkson.

A trifecta!

Parkson was polite, nothing more. He accepted my assurance that the wine was safe, and asked that any further correspondence be sent to his attorney, as he would be out of the country for several weeks. He provided contact information and thanked me for notifying him.

From the tone of Parkson's e-mail I wasn't even sure he knew Gregory had been murdered. Sometimes the weekend people in Pine Ridge could be incredibly oblivious. They didn't seem to understand that their vacation home was in a place where other people lived year-round. It was as though the town ceased to exist between their visits.

Gregory's murder had occurred while Parkson was away, so for him it never happened.

Either the man was incredibly devious, or he really didn't know. I voted for oblivious and moved his name to the bottom of my list.

The computer chimed with an incoming message, drawing my attention back to the screen.

Wineexpert wanted to meet. He suggested Gregory's house, since he understood that was where the wine was stored. He said it would give him the opportunity to see for himself, on behalf of all the partners, that the wine was receiving proper care.

This was what I'd been hoping for. To meet the person behind the anonymous domain name, the one partner whose name wasn't readily apparent.

I agreed to meet him that afternoon. He knew where the house was, and said he would be there at five thirty.

I answered his e-mail, saying I would meet him there, but I got no response. Apparently, wineexpert was now offline.

I called Wade.

Having a trustworthy boyfriend can be a truly wonderful

thing. Wade suggested we get to the house early, and didn't flinch at the idea of going inside. I think he was as curious about the wine cellar as Wineexpert.

I told him about the van, still parked in Mom's garage. It was a detail I hadn't mentioned before, and it elicited a chuckle. "Are you *sure* you don't want to join the sheriff's office?" he asked.

I laughed and told Wade I'd meet him at Mom's house to pick up the van, then hung up.

For the first time in several days I had a few hours free, and I was determined to make the most of them. I dragged out my notes and my copy of the Uniform Plumbing Code and set to work. After all, I still had a test to take.

Before I left for Mom's, I let the dogs out one last time, and fed them an early dinner. I didn't expect to be long, but I had no way to be sure and hungry dogs were more likely to get into trouble.

Why take chances?

Which was precisely what I was doing meeting someone I didn't know in an empty house that belonged to a dead man, to talk about wine that might have been a motive for murder.

I wore my coveralls and ball cap to Gregory's, more out of superstition than necessity, but I let Wade drive the van.

I debated carrying the toolbox. Having Wade along probably negated any camouflage value, but I didn't see any reason to change my routine.

I headed for the bedroom, but Wade stopped in the entry and gave a long, low whistle. I'd forgotten how impressive the house was the first time I saw it, and I had to stop and wait for Wade to recover from his first view of the soaring entry and the glass-walled great room overlooking the manicured backyard.

"You said it was impressive, but I didn't realize just how impressive."

"Yeah. Wait till you see the rest of it."

Wade followed me on a quick tour. I showed him the chilled cabinet I'd found in the kitchen on my first visit.

"This isn't the wine cellar?" he said, walking into the small room. "Seems pretty large to me."

"That's what I thought the first time I saw it, too. But then I started counting the bottles and I realized there were only about a hundred bottles in here. Remember, we figured he had at least a couple hundred *cases* of Veritas wine."

I could see Wade going through the mental calculations. His eyes widened and he looked around the cooler again. "You're right, this is only about a hundred bottles." He looked at me and shook his head. "A couple hundred cases is a *lot* of wine."

"You can't imagine how much," I said.

I led him back through the great room and into the bedroom wing on the far side of the house. This time I didn't hesitate when I came to the door of the master bedroom. I'd already faced that particular demon and it had turned out to be pretty innocuous.

Once inside the room I made a beeline for Gregory's closet. I pointed out the release latches to Wade, and let him do the honors. Much easier on my wrist that way.

With the chest out of the way, I showed him the release for the upper portion of the closet. He triggered the release and swung the upper portion away, marveling at the ingenuity of the construction.

"Well," he said, admiring the work, "I can see why it cost so much to build this. It's pretty amazing."

"Want to see what's inside?" I dangled the key in front of him, then slid it into the lock and opened the door.

I had only been in the room once, and I was nearly as overwhelmed then as Wade was now when we looked inside. The carefully labeled racks covered the walls. There were occasional gaps in the rows, but not many. Each rack was nearly full.

Wade's brain instantly clicked into accountant mode, and I could practically hear the adding machine in his head clicking off the number of racks, rows, and bottles.

I waited while he calculated the total and turned back to look at me. "There are well over two thousand bottles in this room." He looked around, noticing the table and the notebooks for the first time.

He walked over and picked up a notebook labeled "Burgundy" and flipped it open. He understood the organization instantly without explanation.

"It's all cataloged here," he said. "That should make the inventory a lot easier."

"Inventory?"

"Of course. You need to know what's in here, and where it all came from. It's fortunate Gregory keeps such meticulous records." He wandered along the racks, glancing from the book to the shelf and back. "He's always been like that. His tax records are organized and sorted and he files every receipt."

He stopped and looked over at me. "Is that just nerdy of me, that I appreciate how neat and organized he keeps his tax records?"

I shook my head. "I'm sure it made your job a lot easier."

"It does—*did*." He corrected himself, a shadow passing over his face. "I still haven't gotten used to the fact that he's gone."

We had given ourselves an hour, but it quickly became clear that the job of verifying and valuing the collection in Gregory's wine cellar would take several days, at least.

We were about ready to close up and wait for our mystery guest when we heard a voice calling from the entry.

Too late, I realized I hadn't locked the door behind me.

Whispering to Wade to close up the cellar and put everything back in place, I hurried toward the front of the house, in hopes of stalling our visitor until Wade had time to disguise the cellar entrance.

I had considered many possibilities for the position of Wineexpert, but I expected one person, not two.

And I certainly didn't expect either of the two men that confronted me in the dining room.

William Robinson, who had professed no knowledge of Veritas.

And Harry Hamilton, my mother's nosy neighbor.

And they didn't look happy to see me.

chapter 33

"You're Wineexpert?" I asked, looking at Harry Hamilton.

"Oh, please!" William Robinson shook his head. "You think this chump knows anything about *real* wine? I told you before, *I'm* the wine expert."

I stood in the doorway between the dining room and the bedroom wing, trying to block the door without calling attention to the fact.

"Of course," I said to William. "It had to be you—you're certainly knowledgeable enough. I don't know why I didn't see it before now."

Robinson advanced toward the doorway until his belly was nearly touching my padded middle. "What's back there that you don't want us to see?" he asked.

The implied threat in his voice made the hair at the back of my neck stand up. It was a primal fear response, and I trust my instincts.

Robinson was a definite threat.

I stood my ground, blocking the doorway, hoping to give Wade enough time to close up the cellar.

But Robinson wasn't waiting.

He shoved me roughly aside and moved down the hall toward the open bedroom door. He moved pretty fast for a big man, and he was inside the room before I could catch up.

I heard Harry Hamilton scurrying along behind me, but my attention was focused on William. He was clearly the more dangerous of the two, and he was headed directly for the hidden wine cellar.

And Wade.

Robinson followed the sounds coming from Gregory's closet and disappeared inside, with me close behind and Harry Hamilton bringing up the rear.

I reached the door of the closet and stopped. The scene in front of me froze me in place.

Robinson held Wade's right arm twisted high up his back. The pain was obvious on Wade's face as Robinson yanked open the unlocked door of the wine cellar and shoved him inside.

I looked around for a weapon of some kind, but Hamilton shoved me from behind and threw me off balance.

"Get in there," he said, his voice cracking like a twelve-year-old boy.

I regained my footing but in the cramped quarters of the closet I couldn't get turned around to fight back.

Hamilton shoved me again and I stumbled through the door into the wine cellar. Hamilton followed me in.

The cellar, which had seemed spacious before, felt cramped with four people in it, especially when one of the four was William Robinson.

Robinson pushed Wade against the table and released his grip. Wade caught himself before hitting the floor, supporting himself with his uninjured left arm.

We made a great pair with only two good arms between us.

Hamilton stood next to Robinson, the way a toady sticks close to a schoolyard bully for protection. He was quite brave as long as he had Robinson to back him up.

Things fell into place: Hamilton watching the house, Robinson's contempt for Gregory's investments, and his haughty denials about Veritas.

What I had dismissed as arrogance and self-importance was really a guilty conscience.

"You've been a part of Veritas all along, haven't you?"

Robinson glared. "Mr. Hamilton was a member of the Veritas Partnership, not me. I refused to be a party to this so-called investment scheme."

I didn't believe him for a second.

Robinson looked around the room, taking in the racks of wine. His eyes glowed with the intensity of a man beholding a religious shrine.

Clearly, William Robinson worshipped wine.

"Don't move," he snarled at Wade. "You, either." He looked at me.

Robinson moved along the racks, keeping one eye on me and Wade as he pulled occasional bottles from the rack and inspected the labels.

I gauged the distance between me and Robinson. I knew I could put up a good fight if I got a clear shot, and I hadn't seen either man display a weapon.

I shifted my weight and Robinson whirled to confront me. "I said *don't move*." He looked back at Wade. "Can you talk some sense into your girlfriend here? Because if you can't someone is going to get hurt."

Robinson looked back at me. "Move over there next to the Councilman, and stay there." He waited a fraction of a second, then bellowed, "Move! Now!"

I sidled across the floor until I was next to Wade.

Wade reached his right arm out to me and squeezed my hand. There was returning strength in his grip, and I felt the first fluttering of hope.

Between us we might be able to overpower William.

If we did, Hamilton would turn tail and run like the toady he was.

Wade slowly pushed himself away from the table, until he was standing firmly on his own two feet. He tensed. Robinson had caught him off guard and pushed him around, but it wasn't over yet.

Robinson caught the slight movement and turned on

Wade. "I told you not to move or somebody was going to get hurt." His voice was high and tight, close to panic.

I took a step forward and felt bony fingers close over the bandage hidden under the sleeve of my coveralls.

Hot needles shot through my wrist. I gasped in pain.

Wade shot a glance my direction and saw Hamilton's hand wrapped tightly around my damaged wrist. His face burned with anger and he moved toward Hamilton.

"I said not to move," Robinson roared. He raised the bottle he had been inspecting and brought it down on Wade's head.

Wade's eyes rolled back and for an instant I saw only the whites. The world seemed to slow down, and I watched as Wade closed his eyes and sank to the floor.

Robinson turned his blazing eyes to me. "Look what you two made me do! I can't stay here now. It's all your fault!"

He looked past me to Hamilton. "Hold on to her," he commanded as he turned back to the racks and yanked out several bottles.

Robinson stuffed the bottles into a carrier from under the table and moved toward the door.

Hamilton gripped my wrist harder. The pain increased and my knees buckled.

I fought to stay on my feet, but I knew it was only a matter of time before I lost the battle.

Robinson slid past Harry Hamilton and stood in the doorway of the wine cellar.

"Sorry, Harry," he said.

Before Hamilton could react, William was out of the cellar and had slammed the door behind him.

Hamilton pounded on the door in frustration, unable to believe his partner and protector would desert him.

On the other side of the door we could hear the sounds of the closet pieces being slid back into place.

I was locked in a hidden room with an injured man and a useless toady.

And nobody knew we were here.

chapter 34

After several minutes even Harry Hamilton had to admit that we'd been abandoned.

"I can't believe it," he whined. "After everything I did for him."

"Sure," I snarled. The pain in my wrist made me shaky. And really angry. "Like killing Gregory Whitlock."

Hamilton's eye went wide with shock. "I didn't do *that*," he protested.

"Yeah, right." It didn't matter to me which one of them had wielded the knife; they were both involved and they were both guilty.

And they'd been willing to send my mother to prison for the rest of her life to save their own skins.

I had no use for either of them.

Wade stirred and I crouched beside him. He started to sit up, but I put my right hand against his shoulder. "Stay there," I said softly. "You've had a nasty bump on the head. Just stay still, okay?"

He looked up at me, his eyes struggling to focus. "Georgie? What are you doing here?" He glanced around at the unfamiliar surroundings. "What happened?"

"William hit you over the head is what happened." I stopped and drew several deep breaths, regaining control of my anger. "You need to just lay here for a little while," I said, more calmly.

I looked back at Hamilton. He was frantically scrabbling around the door, looking for a way out. Without apparent success.

I left Wade and went back to Hamilton. "Sit!" I commanded. I took his arm in my good right hand and twisted until he crumpled into a sitting position.

"Stay!"

Well, it worked with Buddha, and even sometimes with Daisy. I hoped Hamilton was as smart as an Airedale, though his association with William certainly gave me reason to doubt it.

I rummaged through my pockets until I came up with my cell phone. I flipped it open and checked the screen.

No bars, and I'd let the battery run down to almost nothing.

"Wade?"

"Georgie? What are you doing here?"

The question sent a chill through me. Wade had sustained a nasty blow to the head, and he was acting confused.

Not a good sign.

"I'm trying to get us out of here," I said in a soft voice. "Just wait there and I'll take care of everything, okay?"

Wade nodded, then winced. "Ow!" he said. "That hurts!"

I unzipped my coveralls and struggled out of their tight grip. I had to use both hands, and my wrist throbbed with every movement.

I unwound the padding from around my middle and folded it into a makeshift pillow for Wade. I slipped it under his head, trying to move him as little as possible.

"Just rest here," I said.

I rummaged through his pockets. His cell phone wasn't in his jacket, and I gingerly poked a finger in his pants pocket. His eyes grew wide.

"Just looking for your cell phone," I said, my face flaming.

"Other pocket."

I extracted the phone, trying to have as little actual contact as possible. It might be awkward, but staying locked in this cellar was a lot worse.

Wade's phone at least had a charge, though his signal wasn't much better than mine.

It was all we had.

I punched 9-1-1 and waited. I could hear a faint buzz but I wasn't sure if it was real or if I was only imagining it.

A man's voice answered. I couldn't make out the words.

"Help! We're trapped!" I shouted.

More buzzing on the other end of the line.

I shouted the address. I didn't know if he could hear me any better than I heard him, but I had to try.

The line went dead and I looked at the phone.

Signal lost.

I tried twice more, shouting into the phone until the call dropped and I lost the connection.

I glared at Harry Hamilton. "I don't suppose you have a cell phone?"

He fished in his pocket and retrieved a cheap prepaid phone. But when I flipped it open there was no signal.

Frustration welled up and spilled over onto Hamilton. "What did you think you were doing?" I yelled.

"I was just trying to help William out," he said. "He needed someone to be a go-between for the partnership. He wanted to get hold of some of the wine they were buying, but the only way he could do that was to become part of the group.

"He didn't want to do that, so he offered me a commission to act as his agent. He said there wasn't anything illegal about it."

Hamilton was whining now, trying to justify his involvement with the murder of Gregory Whitlock.

"Whitlock tricked me into telling him I was working for William. He told William he'd expose him to rest of the group if he didn't help him hide those cases. He even offered him a bottle of the wine if he did what Whitlock wanted."

I could imagine Gregory's carrot-and-stick approach. Too bad William Robinson had a sharper stick.

Hamilton shrugged. "William agreed. He wanted that bottle and he insisted on tasting it first. Said it was the best thing he had ever had."

"Did he know it was fake?" I snorted. "Some wine expert! The best wine he ever had, and it wasn't even the real thing. Just impressed by a fancy label and a bunch of lies."

Wade stirred, and I turned around. He has rolled on his side and closed his eyes.

I stepped away from Hamilton and shook Wade's foot. "Don't go to sleep. You have to stay with us."

Wade mumbled and closed his eyes again.

"Wake up!" I yelled.

His eyes opened. He tried to focus on me but I could see the confusion on his face.

"Georgie? What are you doing here? What happened?"

"You got hit, Wade. And you have to stay awake. Okay?"

"Okay," he said. "But I'm really tired."

Fear sent my pulse racing. Wade had a concussion and people with concussions weren't supposed to sleep.

"You can sleep later. Just stay awake a little longer."

"I'll try," he said. He opened his eyes wide and stared at the ceiling.

I turned back to Hamilton. "So Robinson tasted the fake wine." I thought for a second. "That must have been the glass that was on Mom's counter.

"But if he liked it, why kill Gregory?"

"William's just high strung," Hamilton said. There was something in his voice, affection tinged with sadness. "It was an accident. Whitlock told him they had to hide the wine because it was a fake and he couldn't let the appraiser see it. He ridiculed William because he couldn't tell the difference. William just lost his temper. First being suckered in with a fake and then having to cover it up . . ."

"You and William," I wondered aloud, "you're old friends?"

"Since junior high," Hamilton said proudly.

Like being friends with a bullying murderer was something to brag about.

There was one more thing I needed to know.

"My car?" I asked.

Hamilton's misery was all the answer I needed.

"He tried to kill me, too," I said. "And Paula Ciccone."

In the distance I heard voices.

It sounded like someone was in the house.

It couldn't be William. He wasn't coming back, no matter what Harry Hamilton thought.

It had to be the sheriff.

"In here!" I yelled.

I waved at Hamilton and he started screaming, too. Even Wade yelled, though I don't think he quite understood why.

The sound came closer. More than one voice.

Hamilton and I pounded on the walls, trying to attract the attention of our rescuers.

We could hear the voices on the other side of the wall, calling to us. We called back and slammed our fists on the door.

I heard a shout and the sound of the chest rolling away from the wall. Without the key, Robinson had left the door unlocked and put the fixtures back in place over it.

Seconds later the door opened and Fred Mitchell looked in.

"Something I can do for you, Ms. Neverall?"

chapter 35

Everyone tried to talk at once.

I put my fingers in my mouth and whistled.

Several deputies and firemen covered their ears as the piercing sound echoed against the walls of the room.

Silence descended.

"He was part of it," I said to the sheriff, pointing at Harry Hamilton. "And the other part was William Robinson. He hit Wade." I gestured to my boyfriend—definitely my boyfriend—still lying on the floor.

A couple paramedics pushed through the knot of uniforms and knelt next to Wade.

"Careful," I called. "He's had a hard blow to the head, and he's acting confused. I think he has a concussion."

Mitchell fought back a grin. "Any other orders, Ms. Neverall?"

"Find Robinson," I snapped. "He killed Gregory, and he tried to kill me." I waved toward Hamilton, now standing between two of Mitchell's deputies. "Ask him. He and Robinson are old pals. Mom's dear neighbor knows all about it.

"And he was willing to have her go to jail for what he and Robinson did."

Mitchell looked at Hamilton, who obligingly began babbling about how it was all Robinson's fault. Mitchell stopped him and read him his rights, but it made no difference to Hamilton.

He was still blabbering as the deputies cuffed him and led him from the wine cellar.

A few minutes later the paramedics put Wade on a stretcher and took him out, too.

Mitchell looked at me and cocked an eyebrow. "I'm going to need a statement." He sighed. "Come down to the station with me and let's get this over with."

I thought about asking him to let me drive myself, then thought better of it. I was going to need all the good will I could muster before I got to the end of my story.

At least he let me ride in the front seat.

epilogue

It took a few weeks to sort everything out. Mom decided she didn't want to move into Gregory's house alone. Once the estate was probated she planned to sell it. In spite of what had happened, she was staying put in the house where she had lived since I was a little girl.

There was something comforting in knowing she would still be there. I suppose I should have felt some regret about not buying the house, but it was my mother's house and she belonged there, not me. Living in that house was part of my past. It was time I looked to the future.

Robinson had been caught driving his own car, just a few miles away. Hamilton had been right, Robinson was high strung and impulsive. He'd left Gregory's with an armload of rare wine, climbed in his car, and started driving. He was easy to find. The knife he used to kill Gregory was also easy to find—he'd left it in his trunk. The bloodstains were still on it along with his fingerprints.

With my exams completed—and successfully—I threw a party to celebrate, and invited everyone I knew.

Even my mother.

Mom showed up with a large box, which Fred Mitchell carried in from the car for her.

"This is from Gregory," she said softly. She choked up a little, but blinked back the tears and continued, "It isn't really worth a thousand dollars a bottle, but just for to-night, let's pretend it is."

We opened the wine and drank a toast to Gregory.

And to Mom's freedom.

Wade's arm was warm around my waist, holding me tight against him. Dr. Cox had given him an unconditional release earlier in the week, and the wine was only the be-ginning of what I expected might be a long night of cele-bration.

The dogs were learning to adjust to overnight guests.

These were my friends, and my family, the people who stood by me. Sue and Frank, Barry and Paula, my mother. Even Deputy Carruthers showed up briefly. He'd given me the name and number of his friend in Sandy but we both knew the 'Vette might be a lost cause.

I would miss my toy if it couldn't be repaired, but the love I'd found in Pine Ridge would always be here.

Mom poured another round, and clapped her hands, demanding everyone's attention. She thanked all of them, even Frank and Carruthers, for their help and support. The wink she gave the two lawmen displayed a sense of hu-mor I hadn't seen in many years.

Then she turned to me.

"Georgie," she said. Not Georgiana, *Georgie*, like one of my friends. "Thank you. You did far more than any mother could ask, and I will forever be grateful."

She turned back to address the whole room, and with genuine pride, she proposed another toast.

To my new status as a real plumber.

plumbing tips

Eleven Steps for Working on a Leaking or Sluggish Faucet:

WARNING: Before doing any work, turn off the water at the fixture shutoff valves or at the main shutoff valve. Open the faucet to drain the pipes.

1. Determine what type of faucet you're working on. Older faucets are usually compression type. Newer faucets are washerless, and come in disc, valve, ball, and cartridge styles. Models vary by manufacturer, so it's important to get the correct parts.

2. Use penetrating oil before trying to loosen parts with a wrench.

3. Wrap the jaws of your wrench with tape to prevent them from scratching the finish.

4. Plug the drain to prevent small parts from falling down the drain.

5. Line the sink with a towel. If you drop a tool or part you won't damage the sink.

6. Lay out the parts in order as you disassemble the faucet. That way they will be in the proper order when you want to reassemble them.

7. Examine parts for wear and breakage. Remove and mark the space of any broken or worn ones.

8. Take distressed parts to hardware store and purchase replacements.

9. Reassemble faucet in order, incorporating new parts as needed.

10. Slowly restore water to the reassembled faucet. If it still leaks, turn off water, disassemble, and try applying Teflon tape to the joints.

11. If it still leaks, call a plumber!

THE NEWEST CHAPTER IN THE
NEW YORK TIMES BESTSELLING
BOOKTOWN MYSTERIES FROM

LORNA BARRETT

CHAPTER & HEARSE

Mystery bookstore owner Tricia Miles has been
spending more time solving whodunits than
reading them. Now a nearby gas explosion has
injured Tricia's sister's boyfriend, Bob Kelly,
the head of the Chamber of Commerce, and
killed the owner of the town's history bookstore. Tricia's never been a fan of Bob, but when
she reads that he's being tight-lipped about the
"accident," it's time to take action.

M770T0910

M769T0910